"Do you mind?" Joe asked, drawing the strap of her bathing suit off her shoulder.

Susannah didn't say no. Didn't say anything. Her breath was caught somewhere between her heart and mouth. Maybe his hands on her body had captured it. She gasped as he touched his lips to her soft skin.

"You're burning."

She was. She was on fire.

Joe knelt and filled his palm with suntan lotion. He began with her foot, then brushed his fingers up her legs. "Susannah, I don't want to sneak around. Not with you."

"It'd be like having a secret affair," she murmured. "I'm not ashamed. But what others might think . . ."

"An affair," he muttered. "Clandestine. Dangerous." His hands caressed her arms, her shoulders, her back with the honey-smooth lotion.

"Very dangerous," she said softly.

"Exciting?" he asked as he smeared dabs across her cheeks like war paint.

She nodded. Maybe it was the way she licked her lips, but Joe realized that lotion wouldn't work there. His mouth might. Her breath came in short gasps as he pulled her to him, imprisoning her in his arms.

Was it the sun that made skin sizzle against skin?

WHAT ARE *LOVESWEPT* ROMANCES?

They are stories of true romance and touching emotion. We believe those two very important ingredients are constants in our highly sensual and very believable stories in the *LOVESWEPT* line. Our goal is to give you, the reader, stories of consistently high quality that may sometimes make you laugh, sometimes make you cry, but are always fresh and creative and contain many delightful surprises within their pages.

Most romance fans read an enormous number of books. Those they truly love, they keep. Others may be traded with friends and soon forgotten. We hope that each *LOVESWEPT* romance will be a treasure—a "keeper." We will always try to publish

LOVE STORIES YOU'LL NEVER FORGET
BY AUTHORS YOU'LL ALWAYS REMEMBER

The Editors

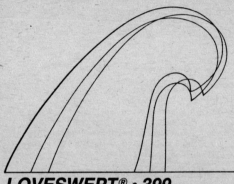

LOVESWEPT® • 399

Terry Lawrence
The Outsider

 BANTAM BOOKS
NEW YORK • TORONTO • LONDON • SYDNEY • AUCKLAND

THE OUTSIDER

A Bantam Book / May 1990

LOVESWEPT® *and the wave device are registered trademarks of Bantam Books, a division of Bantam Doubleday Dell Publishing Group, Inc. Registered in U.S. Patent and Trademark Office and elsewhere.*

If you would be interested in receiving protective vinyl covers for your Loveswept books, please write to this address for information:

Loveswept
Bantam Books
P.O. Box 985
Hicksville, NY 11802

ISBN 0-553-44028-4

Published simultaneously in the United States and Canada

Bantam Books are published by Bantam Books, a division of Bantam Doubleday Dell Publishing Group, Inc. Its trademark, consisting of the words "Bantam Books" and the portrayal of a rooster, is Registered in U.S. Patent and Trademark Office and in other countries. Marca Registrada. Bantam Books, 666 Fifth Avenue, New York, New York 10103.

PRINTED IN THE UNITED STATES OF AMERICA

OPM   0 9 8 7 6 5 4 3 2 1

My thanks to the people of the Grand Traverse Band of Ottawa and Chippewa Indians for their help with the vocabulary. Any misspellings are strictly my own.

One

With a whisper made to accompany a lover's caress, Susannah Moran closed her eyes and sighed. "Come on, baby, do it for me one more time."

Standing at the end of the craps table in the Manitou Lodge Casino, chips piled in front of her, Susannah touched one die under each ear as if dabbing on perfume. Lightly she stroked them down the deep V neckline of her dress, where a breathtaking plunge met the black velvet cummerbund at her waist. There, with trembling hand pressed flat to her abdomen, she switched dice.

Her left hand made the trip back up. Along with every male eye at the table. "Will you do it for Mama once more?" she cooed, kissing the cubes. With a shake, a grin, and a "Come on, seven!" she raised her hand to throw.

The grip that stopped her wrist was warm, firm, and not about to let go. One thought raced through her mind as she slowly turned. At least their security was alert. And quick.

And heart-stoppingly handsome. The man who held her arm was dark, compact, and tough-looking. His eyes were as deceivingly blue as his hair was coal black. He was definitely Native American, Ottawa or Ojibwa. From appearances, years of outdoor life had tanned and weathered his already-dark skin. Judging from the assurance with which he wore the tuxedo, that life had been lived elsewhere.

"Fresh dice, Rick," he said, never taking his eyes off Susannah.

"Yes, sir," the croupier replied.

The man's voice was low, as smooth as the green felt that chafed beneath Susannah's palm as she leaned back on the table, contemplating him.

"Come with me?" he asked suggestively, leaning intimately close—any closer and their bodies would touch.

My, he did this well, she thought, feeling somewhat breathless. She'd never been caught so fast. Not that she'd admit that right away. Nevertheless, he made taking her into custody look downright seductive, a bold new come-on.

The steady buzz around the table continued uninterrupted. No one else realized he was one step away from arresting her. Between them signals were being sent, received. They were the only people in the room who knew exactly what was going on. For some reason the wordless communication made her skin tingle. Everywhere.

As long as she played it cool, she calculated, they'd both be spared a scene. For that she was grateful.

Lifting her chin a notch, she swept back a cascade of red hair and glanced him up and down. "I'd come with you anytime," she said, her voice almost a purr.

His eyes actually darkened, and the pulse in her

wrist accelerated. His fingers found it and squeezed gently. He smiled.

Susannah wanted to run. A rush of butterflies sank like stones in her stomach. This had to be more than just his way of removing her from the game room. An unwelcome thought occurred to her. She'd been caught before while doing her job testing business security; shoplifting, cheating, even picking dollar bills from the till. Although she'd whined, begged, and cried, she'd never offered a bribe. Or been given the chance to make one. Was the appreciative look in his eyes an invitation? At what price would he let her go?

He skimmed her hammering pulse with his thumb. The price was her.

She twisted her wrist in his grip. She felt faint and dizzy and a trifle sick. She wasn't a professional cheat, after all. She was an accountant. Testing how companies treated customers who were caught cheating them was a small part of her duties. It wasn't as if she did it every day. Maybe she could explain. The rocketing pulse had to be a dead giveaway. She twisted again, noticing the rasp of his calluses against her skin.

Quietly ordering play to resume, he released her arm and indicated the way with a sweep of his hand. As he guided her through the three-deep crowd at the table, she made a show of kissing the dice good-bye and tried tossing them back on the table. "Keep these warm for me, doll."

"Uh-uh," the man said, his voice just behind her ear. "I'll hold on to those. Might bring me luck."

On the outside Susannah pouted, although she never thought she did that well. She told herself it was what her imitation sophisticated lady would do. Plunking the dice in his hand, she turned. "Are we going somewhere?"

Jail, if she was lucky, she thought grimly. An evening of very long explanations stretched before her.

"Let's try the bar," he said instead. "I'd like to buy you a drink." He smiled again. He had white shark teeth, and a devilish glint in his eye, which, under other circumstances, would have set warning bells off in Susannah's head. In reality it was more like air raid sirens.

He was certainly taking his time about arresting her. Could it be he had other things in mind? Things that merely began with buying a woman a drink? Staring into eyes as blue and unflinching as polished steel, she wouldn't have pegged him as so easily corrupted. Familiar with the temptations perhaps, but somehow beyond them.

"Nicky, the usual," he said to the bartender, "and for the *lady*?" The glint in his eye made it clear he was granting her that much, for now.

Suddenly parched, Susannah said the first thing that came to mind. "Diet red pop."

Her host's look of surprise was matched with a rumbling laugh. It reminded her of a lion settling down to sleep, pleased after a kill. She groaned inwardly. This was going to be a very long night indeed.

She studied him while they waited for their drinks, his smile revealing a roadmap of lines. The Native American background or years in the sun, she wondered for the second time. He had the general build of the reservation Indians she'd seen in Northern Michigan—stocky, wide-shouldered, not much taller than she was. His nose was aquiline, his cheekbones broad and sharp. And those blue eyes. He was as suave as any corporate exec on the lookout for a takeover. And as dangerous.

The tux said sophisticated and smooth. The calluses, earthy and rugged. The eyes . . . He looked away.

Collecting their drinks, he paid for hers and nodded toward an unused poker table in a far corner. "Shall we sit?"

Following the subtle sway of her hips, Joe had to admit the woman moved well. "Tell me something I don't already know," he muttered to himself. He'd kept an eye on her from the moment he'd spotted her. The floor-length shimmering red dress she wore would have been noticed in the swankest club in Vegas, not to mention the body inside it. In this bingo-palace-turned-casino on a reservation in northern Michigan, the flashy evening wear had drawn stares all night.

He suspected it was meant to. Like the obvious titillating motion with the dice down the front of her dress, it snagged attention while her other hand brought out a second pair from the folds of material at her waist. Clever, smoothly done, supremely distracting. Like the way his heart thudded in his chest every time he looked at her.

It had been a while since a woman had elicited so primal a response in him. It didn't take much reminding to remember that flashy redheads such as this one were a sure-fire dead end. On top of that she'd been caught red-handed. He swallowed his anger and got down to business.

When they got comfortable in their chairs, he took a sip of his drink. Nicky had given him his usual, a scotch so watered down, Joe could have nursed it all night. Looking at her, he wished it were a full-strength double.

Aimlessly, he twirled the confiscated dice on the poker-table surface. Her eyes went straight to them. Would a professional cheat be that obvious, he wondered. She might be foolish. She might be drunk. She might be fronting for someone else— the ultimate distraction. Any way he looked at it, she was trying to cheat his people. What was left of his drink went down hard.

He tossed the dice her way. Snake eyes. "You like our casino?" he asked, noting the flush on her cheeks.

"Do you work here?"

"Did you think I was picking you up?"

On a number of charges, Susannah thought wryly. She shrugged, vainly attempting a bored, too-sophisticated-for-words wave of her hand. She'd been assigned the spoiled-socialite role. She hoped she could pull it off.

The glint in his eye was as hard as the ice in his glass. "You didn't answer my question."

"*Your* casino? It's very nice." It was. So was her eagerness to escape his tenacious stare. Slowly she studied the room.

The Manitou Lodge looked as if it had been designed for a nineteenth-century lumber baron and decorated with local Indian crafts. Heavy beams crossed the cavernous two-story room, deer-antler chandeliers hung at intervals separated by gently moving brass fans. Indian blankets, baskets, and quill designs dotted the walls. Two massive stone fireplaces were set at either end. Low crackling fires hissed in their grates, mostly for show on this early summer night. In the looming space sat mahogany tables covered with dark green felt and clattering roulette wheels.

Card dealers wore white shirts, black suspenders, and dark green bow ties. Pit bosses wore dark green cummerbunds and slacks with black satin stripes down the sides. The man across from Susannah wore a tux. Exactly what was he in the scheme of things? "Mind telling me who's buying me this drink?"

"Compliments of the house."

"That would make you the famous Manitou Lodge. May I call you Manny for short?"

He smiled again. Barely. "Joe Bond."

"Susannah Moran. Chicago." She reached out a perfectly manicured hand. He released it after a pause, then watched her fingernails tap nervously against her glass.

Red nails, red dress, red pop, he noted, but none had a thing on that mane of red hair. If he didn't stick to the subject at hand, he could find himself more than a little aroused. "You're a tourist, then."

"Aren't most of your customers?"

He nodded. "Tourists and locals." None of whom came dressed like this one. The ambience was strictly casual.

"Is this your regular job?" she asked.

"No." Maybe she'd been casing the place, Joe speculated, trying to catch it on a night when the regulars were off. "No, it's not."

"You're not very talkative. I find that remarkable for an official host."

"I help out two nights a week."

"Volunteer work? In a casino? Now, that's a combination!"

Her laughter glittered like her smile, easy and sparkling. The polish wasn't only on her nails. Joe had seen the type during his years in business. She'd look good on any man's arm, carelessly spending any man's money. But something about her didn't click. The flutter of nerves? The red pop? He sensed vulnerability—or was that an act too? Maybe he should shake her up again. "I wanted you to be the one to answer questions."

She took another swallow, unaware the pop was staining her lips a fruity red. "Is that so?"

He didn't answer.

She tried to sip in a convincingly sophisticated, indifferent manner. She suspected his silence could go on forever. Not so hers. "And what do you do the other five nights a week?"

"Is that an offer?"

"I meant for your real job." She peered intently at her drink.

She was blushing. Now, that was a surprise. Joe watched the color in her cheeks deepen, then subside. "I have a fishing charter."

"Oh. That explains—" She stopped herself from saying "the calluses." She didn't want him to know she'd noticed, or that she still felt them. "That explains the tan," she said.

"I'm three-quarters Ottawa. That explains the tan."

"Oh." She was attempting, a little desperately, to cultivate a polite, tepid tone, not to be drawn in by his intensity or his humor. One minute she was sure he saw through her, the next they were trading more small talk.

"How long will you be visiting?"

"Just got here." She shrugged.

"Staying?"

"At the condos down the way."

Anyone would have thought they were strangers passing the time.

"On the waterside?" he asked.

"Yes," she practically hissed. Any more chitchat and she'd scream. *Arrest me, dammit! Do something! Just get to the point!*

"Nice place," was all he said. "Expensive."

Her nails tick-tocked against her glass. Enough of this cat-and-mouse game. Someone had to get to the point. "Your casino is very well run. Very discreet." Her brown eyes met his gaze and held it.

Hefting the dice again, he let them fall. Two fours. "You were winning a lot over there."

"I'm lucky. Sometimes." She tossed her hair. Absently fingering the V neck, she caught him staring at the freckles between her breasts, and she stopped. The dice on the table read boxcars.

His turn to catch her looking. He lifted a brow as if to say, "Well?"

"Are you accusing me of cheating?" she blurted out.

He kept his face immobile, although he wanted very badly to smile just then. He liked that hint of innocence. Any more of it and she might convince him she didn't do this every time she walked into a casino.

"If you don't mind, I think I'll return to the tables." She drained her drink and prepared to leave.

Almost imperceptibly, he shook his head no. She stayed. "I'm not accusing you of anything. Not without proof."

"The dice aren't loaded." Of that she was sure. "It's the way you're tossing them. You keep touching them. Manipulating them."

"That could apply to a lot of things. Men. Women." Her blush was furious now, matching her glare. Okay, he'd drop the innuendos. "What about the other pair of dice?" he asked.

They weren't loaded either, Susannah knew, but convincing him it was just a test of their customer relations would take too much explaining. "I'm afraid I don't know what you're talking about—"

He pulled his chair closer to hers. Their knees

bumped, but it was no accident. His thigh stayed close, his arm stretched across the back of her chair. With what little breath Susannah had left, she distinguished the scent of musky after-shave and alcohol.

"Let me put it this way," he said, his fingers tracing the deep V that also defined the back of her dress. He detected gooseflesh up and down her spine. "If I were to search you," he murmured in her ear, "what would I find?"

This close her eyes were deep brown, fringed with long sable lashes. They also indicated she was frightened, a little aroused, and more than a little furious. "The dice aren't loaded."

"Which ones?"

She grasped his hand before he could move it around to the front of her dress. "I have no idea who you are or what function you perform here, but I know you have no legal authority to search me."

"Especially not here on the floor of the casino. Not that I wouldn't enjoy that."

"If you can't keep your hands to yourself, I'm afraid I'll have to leave," she announced primly, rising unsteadily.

Firmly gripping her elbow, his voice remained low. "You're right. I have no authority. But unless you want to be turned over to those who do, you'll answer a few more questions."

She couldn't reveal who she was, not yet. Jack, her boss, hadn't played his part as an unruly drunk yet. Explaining the test now would put all the employees on alert. With a growing sense of panic, Susannah shook off Joe's hand and headed for the exit. The FBI itself could get into the act; anything was better than further contact with this man.

Her back to him, she remembered to walk tall, not run. There'd been more than one time in her life lately when that simple rule had kept her chin above water.

Joe stayed by her side. "All right, then," he said reasonably, "I'll walk you to your car."

She fumbled with her black clutch bag. "My chips."

"I'll hold on to them for you."

"What if I don't come back?"

"I don't expect you will."

Her mouth dropped. Joe detected another crack in the facade. Why was she doing this? Did she need the money that badly? From the look of her, he doubted she knew what true poverty was.

"You can't keep my chips," she said. "Regulations—"

"I know," he interrupted curtly. If she knew the regs that well, she had done this before. "That's why I said I'd hold them for you until you came back."

Neat. Despicable but neat. Susannah actually found a reservoir of imitation outrage. "I must say it's been a lovely evening. Good night." Flouncing onto the deck outside, she hoped he'd accept it as the full-scale retreat it was.

She wasn't getting away that easy. He followed her along the deck railing to a shadowy corner. She made a show of looking for her car in the crammed parking lot.

Why was he tailing her if he didn't mean to arrest her? The possibility that he was fishing for a bribe returned. Although it wasn't part of the test, management would certainly want to know if a staff member was crooked. The danger was in discovering how far *she* was willing to go to find out.

Taking a deep breath, she turned, spreading her hands on the rail behind her. "Do you really want me not to come back?" It was as sultry as she could make it. She almost choked as he stepped closer, his body inches from hers. Suddenly she didn't care if he was corrupt. Flirting was fun. Teasing could get nasty.

The sodium parking lights did nothing for her fair skin. An angry and uncharitable part of Joe made him want to tell her so. He knew what she was up to, bribing him with her body. The anger didn't stop his body from reacting, urging her back into the shadows. "Why don't you stay right here?"

Her skin quivered when he touched her shoulders. So did his. She was a cheat, his mind all but shouted. Bad news. Why that didn't stop him from wanting to kiss her he'd never know.

"Will you let me go?" she asked, meaning would he let her get away with it. The problem was, she asked it in such a way that letting her go was the last thing any sane man would do.

Joe turned her face up with his fingertips. The skin under her chin was as soft as that on her wrist, warmed from the blood coloring her cheeks.

"Joe?"

From her parted lips his name came out in a whisper that made his stomach tighten. Another part of his body throbbed and grew hot. He didn't know if that was her heartbeat or his, pounding in his ears like a drum in a forest. His lips brushed hers. She turned her head, but he found her lips again. She made a sound like a no, but her mouth quickly, surprisingly, softened under his.

His hand went around her waist, pulling her in tight. She stiffened when body touched body. Joe was too busy to notice, his hand sliding around the front of her dress to the black velvet cummerbund and the two small lumps of hidden dice.

Susannah gasped in outrage and tore her mouth from his.

"Anyone would have thought I'd been taking liberties." His laugh was as cold as his eyes. "Maybe I should turn you over to the tribal police now."

"Joe, please. Let me go. I'll explain it all in a few days."

Days? Joe knew she'd be long gone by then. "And what will you give me in return?"

She swallowed a shot of acid in the back of her throat. The kiss had been wonderful. Almost enough to make her forget the man who'd given it to her. "You want a cut of the action?"

"What I want you can't give me." He moved in closer, his body blatant and hard. "Not in public, anyway."

So he was after what every other man was after, to use her grandmother's trite phrase. Susannah recovered her poise and stepped out of his arms, a little surprised when he let her go. She raised her chin. "You'll get everything that's coming to you, Joe," she said tartly. "Meet me here Wednesday night." The results of the test would be announced to the tribal council Wednesday afternoon. She'd be quite surprised if he dared show his face after that.

"All right," he replied. The ice-queen act was back. That didn't stop her from practically running to her car. What would it hurt to let her go? She was leaving with nothing and she wouldn't be back. He ought to consider himself lucky. She was definitely the wrong kind of woman for him.

Wiping his lips with the back of his hand, he knew it had been a close call.

• • • •

Two hours later, well past midnight, the encounter with the woman in red still gnawed at him. He opened the door to the back office. "William, what the hell is going on here?"

William Missaukee sat behind the cramped desk. A chipped metal desk light cast harsh shadows across his deep brown face. "Problem on the floor, Joe?"

"Too many problems. First there was the drunk."

"Get rid of him?"

"Nicki did."

William glanced up at his harsh tone.

"Very smoothly," Joe amended.

The flicker of concern faded in William's otherwise unreadable black eyes. Joe always figured that was his greatest asset as council chief; he kept his opinions to himself and gave very little away.

"So what's bothering you, Joe?"

"A loudmouth followed."

"They're so rare?"

"This one started an argument about the blackjack decks. Said they were opened, marked, and resealed."

"You handle that one?"

"Easily."

"Liquor and gambling means drunks and disgruntled losers."

"Then there was the matter of the loaded dice. And a loaded dame to go with them."

"Alcohol again?"

"Not that kind of loaded."

William permitted himself a small smile. He'd seen the woman in question. "Pretty, eh?"

"More stacked than a crooked deck of cards."

"You got a problem with that, Joe?"

Joe ticked off the problems on one hand. "I

know we're growing, it's early summer, and all the *touristas* are hitting town at once, but even for us that's a lot of trouble for one night."

"Full moon?" the older man asked disingenuously

Joe cursed, but kept it quiet out of respect.

"Maybe we should chart our problem nights and see how they match," William said. "I've heard the time of the month does make a difference in Vegas."

"Do the feds have a form we could fill out on it?"

Joe's remark hit its target like a sharp arrow.

The federal government had been seeking ways to shut down reservation gambling for close to ten years, five in the case of this reservation. If the operation wasn't scrupulously clean, it would be closed and the tribe would lose its best means of supporting its people.

"I'm wondering if somebody is trying to set us up," Joe suggested. "Make it look like we can't run things ourselves."

Joe always had been quick. Intuitive too. William sighed. "Perhaps I should tell you about the lady in the red dress."

Two

On Wednesday afternoon Susannah was prepared for the presentation to the tribal council. Seeing Joe Bond sitting on the council was a nasty shock. Joe merely nodded and went back to reading the reports passed out before hand.

"He's on the council?" Susannah whispered hurriedly to Jack.

Jack Hainford, senior partner at Whitman, Jablonski, and Parritt, leaned across their table, mistaking her urgency for nerves. "Just give your report. You'll do great."

"But what about the test results?"

He shrugged and opened his palms to the ceiling. "I'm lending silent support this time out. Spring 'em whenever you're ready."

Susannah knew being chosen to present the audit proposal was a feather in her cap—unless they failed to win the account, in which case her reputation at the Chicago office could hardly slip any further. After an unpleasant incident involving a major account, she'd offered to resign. They'd given her this assignment instead.

At a nod from William Missaukee, she took a sip of water, reminded herself not to rush, and began. "As you are no doubt aware, your casino operation has grown too complex for the present accountants, which is why they've asked to be replaced. Too many government forms having to be prepared and sent to too many conflicting agencies. In addition, there are multiple investments being made within the tribe itself. You wish to design and fund an infrastructure for further economic development, including housing and job opportunities for your members. For all these you require expertise, hands-on procedural streamlining, and sound but innovative financial advice. I believe our firm, Whitman, Jablonski, and Parritt, would represent your interests to the fullest."

Joe was looking at her, had been since she'd begun speaking. She couldn't let it rattle her. She smoothed down the gray and black tweed skirt and nervously wiped a ticklish strand of hair off the jacket's black velvet collar. If anything, he should be the one who was nervous. She made a point of making eye contact with every other council member. "Please feel free to ask questions at any time."

"Could you expand on the innovative methods?" Missaukee asked.

"Testing, for one." Susannah's gaze rested on Joe Bond for a fraction of a second. This was it. "Whitman, Jablonski, and Parritt tests every company it proposes to audit and those that need our accounting services. Before we acquire the account, we go in pretending to be customers—difficult ones, demanding ones—and see what kind of treatment we get. The bottom line isn't money but how well you serve your customers. All profits follow from that."

"And the lodge?"

"In two out of three instances, one drunk customer and one who was obnoxious—"

Jack chuckled at his role in it.

"—the treatment of difficult customers was excellent. There was, however, one employee, Mr. Bond"—Susannah nodded his way but didn't meet his stare—"who intimated that he would be willing to look the other way after he caught me switching dice at the craps table."

The tension in the room escalated with murmurs of surprise as board members took sidelong glances at Joe.

"In exchange for what?" Missaukee asked.

Susannah clenched her hands at her side, determined not to blush. "In exchange for sexual favors."

Joe's voice, as low and husky as thick green felt, sounded from the end of the table. "Anytime, Miss Moran."

Enduring a round of locker-room laughter, Susannah felt every gaze evaluating her. Only William Missaukee remained aloof. Lifting his palm, he quieted the council. "I take it he never received this bribe?"

"No, sir. I suggested Wednesday night, knowing we'd be meeting today."

"Can't believe you missed out on that one, Joe," Missaukee remarked lightly.

So much for her ally on the council. Susannah blushed, gritting her teeth. This was exactly how she did not want to be portrayed. Beauty first, ability second.

Missaukee cleared his throat. "Gentlemen, and Miss Moran, I would like to point out that Joe came directly to me about this incident the night it happened. I revealed the lady's identity to him, and we let the matter drop."

Susannah's mouth fell open. *He'd* lured *her* into offering the bribe? They'd both been putting on an act. It took a few minutes of furious paper shuffling before she could continue. Joe's wry smile of triumph didn't help.

She played the businesswoman better than the sophisticate, Joe thought. Interesting woman. The mane of red hair refused to stay as tightly pinned back as she wanted it to. It gave her an excuse to nervously touch the combs that held it in place. His fingers itched to take them out and let it fall.

Nevertheless, he had to admit she was handling the presentation well. Advising without telling. Giving tactful suggestions instead of orders. Not patronizing. All the mistakes he'd made three years before in this same room. He impatiently flipped to the next page when instructed, but his mind was elsewhere.

Not so long ago he'd walked into this room with a college degree, eight years experience and business savvy from the white man's world, and proceeded to tell the council exactly what needed to be done. He'd been stunned at the polite but resolutely cold shoulder he'd received.

It was his mother who had sat him down a few days later. "I've lived here all my life," she'd said. "You only summers."

That had been the arrangement after his parents' divorce. Later, after his fast-track business career had begun, visits to the reservation dwindled to long weekends.

He'd made millions for others, had been the token Native American on more than one payroll, had hobnobbed with women just like Susannah Moran—career-oriented, sharp, quick to step up to an opportunity or walk away from an affair. One had walked away from him. Yet he'd chosen to come back, expecting the joyful greeting reserved for a prodigal son who had all the money and dash of a successful entrepreneur. No one had listened.

His mother's words still stung. "You act as if you know more than us because you've been out in the *real* world. The casino, the developments, this is about *us* doing things *our* way. No one wants to be told what to do anymore."

"So what do I do?" Joe asked. "I can't sit by and look at all this. The poverty alone would kill anyone's spirit. At least let me buy you a better place."

Three years later, remembering the chilly look in her eyes, he flinched with shame. "I live with my people, like my people," she'd said.

He'd paced the creaking floors of her mobile home. "I could get results, damnit. I've done it for more than one company."

"This is not a business, it's a community that you're not a part of yet. You have to be patient. Give them time to trust you, to learn that you mean to stay."

So he'd volunteered at the casino, bought a fishing boat, and let them give him an economic grant, because paying it back would mean something, and making it work would mean even more.

The previous year he'd been elected to the council. But he still felt like an outsider.

When he married that might change, his mother said.

If he married.

Until then he was still being tested, and not just by Susannah Moran's accounting firm.

• • •

"Went well," Jack said, holding his tie to his chest as he drank from a water fountain in the hall. "Good job."

"Thanks," she replied.

"Nervous?"

"A little. What do you think our chances are?"

"You heard the other guys' presentations. They're either too small or unwilling to sacrifice a staff member up here for the entire summer."

"Should I be flattered?"

"You know what I mean."

She did. It would get her out of the main office for a few months, away from the memories, the embarrassment.

"We're a shoo-in."

His confidence made Susannah smile. For a man of fifty-five he had all the enthusiasm and go-getting qualities of a business school grad.

"I'm worried that our test may have ruffled some feathers." Joe Bond's in particular.

"They passed with flying colors. They'll like us for making them look good."

Susannah laughed. Jack might be eager, but he wasn't naive. His grasp of politics was unequaled.

The door opened, and they were ushered back inside. With a subtle nod of his head, Missaukee signaled another council member to begin. "The Band of Ottawa and Chippewa Indians would be pleased to have Whitman, Jablonski, and Parritt conduct an audit of our present system and to take over and redesign that system to allow for expansion as future needs dictate. A performance evaluation will be conducted each year before the contract is renewed."

Jack winked at Susannah and tilted his head toward the council table.

"Of course," Susannah replied, striding forward. "Evaluations are expected."

A half-dozen plans tumbled through her mind as she shook hands with each council member. She'd have to extend the two-week lease on her condo for the entire summer. It would take that long to examine their present methods and institute new procedures. Jack would take the company car back with him to Chicago. She'd have to replace it. Oh, yes, and she'd have to set things right with Joe Bond.

The last was unavoidable. One touch of his hand closing around hers and she was slammed back into the present. The calluses were still there, the lingering grip, the way his gaze brushed across her lips, the buzzing in her veins when she looked at him.

"Welcome aboard," was all he said, his eyes a piercing blue, impenetrable and guarded.

Susannah rolled over in bed, sighed deeply, and smiled at the sunrise. Why did she never see these in Chicago? "Building faces the wrong way," she muttered, licking her teeth. What was a vacation without sleeping in? Ah, but what was a glorious sunrise if it couldn't be enjoyed?

"And who's on vacation?" She chuckled and punched her pillow into a softer pile. It finally hit her that she'd actually be living there for the rest of the summer. In paradise. She grinned at the lightening sky over the smooth water.

"And no more customer relations tests!" With a joyous whoop, she bounded out of bed. Play-acting could be fun. Her ability with people had smoothed out many a tricky moment. But Saturday night at the casino had been too close for comfort. The memory of Joe Bond's mouth on hers and her uninhibited, unexpected, and completely uncalled-for reaction made her want to crawl right back under the covers. She wanted to be nothing but an accountant for a while.

After brushing her teeth, she despaired of her hair, and tossed on a baggy cotton sweater and shorts that looked like men's boxers. She walked out the sliding glass doors to the patio. The condo was marvelous—water frontage, sand beach, deck, fireplace. "In Chicago, half a million at least." And Joe Bond had thought them expensive!

Bond again. She remembered his eyes, his low, persistent voice, the alarms that had gone off all over her skin when she'd walked into the council room and seen him there.

She shivered in the chilly morning air and ran her hands up and down her arms before stepping back inside. It was the circumstances under which they'd met, that's all. Her senses had been heightened by the danger, the deception. The next time she saw him she'd apologize in earnest. Everything would be settled between them. Meanwhile, looking out at the boats bobbing in the marina, she decided to join them.

As the sky turned pink over the peninsula across the bay, she dumped a teaspoon of sugar into her black coffee and tried not to spill it as she hiked over the sand to the boat ramp. She stepped delicately down the floating walkways, past aisles of creaking sailboats, flags flapping, lines tinging against metal masts. She kept her steps quiet, mindful of people who might be sleeping on these floating water beds. She grinned, taking a deep breath and sipping her first cup of coffee of the day. Even TV commercials didn't get this good, she thought.

Feeling a trifle self-conscious, she sat cross-legged in the middle of the walkway and let the morning rays tentatively touch her body. Little shivery strokes of breeze flirted up and down her legs. The sweater was a good idea. "Probably not six A.M. yet," she muttered, surprised that she hadn't so much as glanced at her watch this morning.

Wrapping an arm around one raised knee, she absentmindedly ran her palm up and down her shin. Stubble. Couldn't put off shaving another day, especially not in summer. Idly scratching her back, she chuckled. If Joe Bond could see her now. She hardly appeared the wildly coiffed socialite or the put-together businesswoman. She felt delightfully scruffy with her hair drawn hurriedly back in a ponytail and wearing clothes meant for relaxing in.

Would that her bosses at Whitman, Jablonski never see her this way. Of course, the office affair with Keith had hurt her career in many ways. Winning this account wouldn't offset the blame she'd taken for losing the Showcase account.

Showcase, she thought disdainfully, taking a sip of rapidly cooling coffee. "It would have to have been called that."

She told herself she didn't care, although she'd cared desperately at first, to the point of working herself to exhaustion to prove something she shouldn't have had to prove—her ability, her integrity. If only Keith had stood by her. The coffee tasted bitter, and she swallowed the needling suspicion that Keith was the one who'd pinned the blame on her in the first place.

"Concentrate on this," she murmured, closing her eyes, letting her head fall back, willing herself to relax, to listen to the water lapping against the hulls. She needed this break, this distance. A chance to regain her lost confidence, her reputation, recover from one dreadful mistake—

The clunk of footsteps startled her. She twisted around.

"Mr. Bond! Nice to see you again." Her smile was genuine, relieved. At least she could put one thing right in her life. She prided herself on her ability to make friends. The fact that she'd given him the wrong impression at the casino bothered her, even if it had been for a good reason.

Joe slowed to a stop a good ten feet away. The walkway was narrow. With his arms full of equipment, he knew he couldn't pass, not without touching her.

Every time he saw her she looked different. First the shimmering red dress, next the business suit. This time her hair was pulled back in a ponytail, soft red tendrils wisping across her forehead. He watched her bare legs unfold from the sitting position as she stood, tugging self-consciously at the bottom of her sweater till it hung loosely around her thighs.

If she was different each time, why was his reaction always the same? The tight gut, the pounding heart, the slow, deliberate beat in his veins.

Every damn time.

"I'm sorry about that test," she was saying, her voice whispery and urgent. She was keeping it low because of the boats around them. The excuse didn't dampen his reaction.

"As for the bribery, I had no way of knowing how far you'd go." She shrugged and laughed.

His reply was suggestive yet matter-of-fact. "I was wondering the same about you."

She wasn't wearing a bra. Even though she wore a bulky sweater, he could tell. She might have just gotten out of bed—a warm, rumpled one. Were those boxer shorts? He looked her up and down, slowly, completely, curiously.

But the sun insisted on highlighting every golden strand in her hair, illuminating the rosy flush on her cheeks, the one that looked like afterglow.

Was the fact that they were alone making her this nervous? Was he the cause? She'd be wringing her hands if she didn't have that coffee mug to strangle.

He nodded toward the tightly held cup. "You look like you've been caught doing something you shouldn't."

"Just relaxing," she said brightly, gesturing at the sunrise with her cup. Some coffee sloshed over the rim.

"Is that a crime?"

"Where I come from it might be. Work ethic, you know."

"Big city."

"Small towns too." And everywhere in between, judging from the way her parents pulled up stakes. "Peace pipe?" She extended her hand, then quickly withdrew it. "Uh, sorry."

"We do have some sense of humor," he replied, setting down some of his gear and allowing himself a smile.

She tried not to notice the all-too-attractive glint in his eye.

"Apology accepted, then?" She extended her hand again, looking him straight in the eye.

She had no makeup on, Joe realized. It made her look young, vulnerable. Shoulders back, gaze unwavering, she also looked honest and forthright, a woman a man could trust. When he wasn't busy making love to her from dawn to dusk.

Abruptly dismissing the image, he leaned a fishing pole against his thigh, shook her hand, and let it drop.

"May I help you with any of that stuff?" she asked. Her ponytail bobbed when she nodded toward the pile.

"No need."

"Really, it's the least I can do."

Before he could stop her she had two fishing poles tucked in her armpit and one handle of the big cooler, leaving him to lift the other end.

"Which boat's yours?"

"That one."

Susannah gazed over at the fishing charter. A two-tier affair, it had a raised bridge, radio antennae, padded bench seats, and a couple of pirate trunks for storage. The scrolled writing on the side read *The Sporting Chance.*

"Cute name. All yours?"

"My life and livelihood," he replied, hefting the cooler up on deck.

In a knit top and khaki shorts, he looked younger than he had in their first two meetings. The deep skin tones could easily be mistaken for a tan, if one failed to take into account the wide cheekbones and black hair, a shock of which fell across his forehead as he crouched on the deck.

She wasn't the least tempted to comb it back. Friends—that's all they would be. It was safer. Besides, history had shown that she was better at making friends than picking men.

"Want to come on board?"

"I don't want to disturb you."

"No problem." She'd been disturbing him since they'd met. Joe watched her climb the ladder, reaching out to haul her up the last step. That quickly, she was face-to-face with him. That quickly, he found something to keep him busy. "Gotta get this stuff set up. Want some more coffee?"

She'd left her mug on the dock. "Sure, let me start it." It would keep her busy, stop her from watching him move, walk, crouch, his thick fingers so precisely separating fish hooks in the neatly ordered tackle box.

"It's in the galley there. I've got a coffeemaker."

She ducked through a door. The galley was part kitchen, part fold-down table with a short couch that could double as a bed. Susannah found the coffeemaker and set to work. When Joe blocked the light of the doorway, her hands stopped.

He stood silently, watching what she'd been doing.

"Coffee is in the cupboard over the counter."

"I found it."

"I take mine black." He winked.

"Ah, well, if it's an order, then. Aye-aye."

She sensed him keenly as he came up beside her. His legs were muscled, his hips narrow, delineated by shorts with button-down back pockets. Her mind wasn't on what she was doing; the sugar packet tore in two, scattering crystals everywhere. "Sorry."

"Dustbuster's under the counter."

"Thanks. Your boat seems to have everything."

"All for the customers."

"Is chartering a big business around here?"

"Not bad. I do fishing and sunset tours of the bay, some catered dinners. Because fishing is a traditional means of support for the tribe, I thought I'd introduce the sport-fishing side. It's worked so far."

"What were you involved in before this?"

"Various things."

"You're not very talkative in the morning."

She was chatty and cheerful, and for some reason he knew he ought to explore, he didn't mind it. Not at all.

"Hello in there," she said, teasing him out of his silence.

"Wooden Indian," he mumbled.

Her easy laugh coaxed a smile from him. "You're funnier than you let on, and you've done a lot more than go fishing all your life."

True, but he didn't want to get into it right now. "What about you? When you're not being an accountant, do you make a career out of cheating at dice?"

"Oh, no." She put on a very serious expression. "I usually shoplift."

He laughed in spite of himself and stocked the small fridge with the contents of the cooler. "Get caught a lot?"

"A few times. Of course, that's when the real test begins; how you're treated." For a moment all she could think of was that first touch, his hand on her arm, the slow and easy 'Come with me?' She'd been caught before, but never by a man like him. "Cups?" she asked.

"On top," he answered.

They were two simple words. But by the time she turned to hand him his coffee, they'd started a fantasy galloping through her head, one she had to stop.

"Do you always flirt when cornered?"

Susannah broke the brief eye contact first, her smile replaced by a pucker as she blew on the steaming coffee. She knew he wasn't referring only to Saturday night. The galley was small, narrow, crowded. "I was an army brat," she said, answering his question in a roundabout way. "We lived everywhere. Mom says it broke her heart every time I asked if we were done moving yet. I didn't mean it that way. I just needed to know how much time I had to make friends. I guess flirting, if you want to call it that, kind of speeds things up."

"Guess it does. Especially if you're going to be moving on." He tucked that thought away for future reference.

Susannah could hear movement and noises outside as the marina began to come to life, emphasizing how quiet the galley had grown. A shaft of sunlight poured through the door, throwing Joe's face into shadow—as it had been when he'd moved in so close on the deck outside the casino. His breath on her face was warm then, too, like the heat rising from her coffee.

"Want a napkin?" She moved to grab a couple from the holder on the table. He moved to head outside. They collided and froze, body to body, thigh to thigh. Jumping away was as embarrassing as staying. Susannah didn't move. The boat gently rocked them.

"Excuse me," she said, a breathy sound she barely recognized as her voice. What happened to hale and hearty? Good friends and a helping hand? Those had been lost somewhere, just about the time he touched her.

"In a hurry?" he asked, his tone as gentle and teasing as the look in his eye. He was laughing at her.

And why shouldn't he? She was acting like an overwrought virgin. "I'm not exactly the temptress I was playing the other night."

"No?" He tilted her chin with his fingertips. "You could have fooled me." She did, every time he saw her. Every time he made up his mind to force her out of his thoughts. Then she looked at him with those brown eyes, warm, caring, and smiled.

"I'd like us to be friends."

"Do we have to be?" He didn't want friendship. He wanted the fluttering, excited heartbeat he'd felt under his hand when he'd been searching for those dice, the heartbeat he knew he'd feel right now if he pushed her any further. He could have it, too, as long as he didn't think about the future, or the tribe, or what his people would think if he took up with an outsider. If he blocked everything out of his mind and took her mouth . . .

"Ahoy there, matey!" Men's voices shouted outside.

Joe grimaced.

Susannah took a gulp of air. For a moment she was sure he was going to—

Glancing over his shoulder, she saw men standing on the dock.

"Weekend sailors," Joe muttered. "After you."

Susannah stepped out first, blinking in the light. The escape was as narrow as the space they'd been standing in.

A low whistle met her as she emerged to the appreciative gaze of three college buddies.

"Ho ho ho!"

"I'd trade my bottle of rum for that!"

"Looks like we interrupted something, hey?"

Susannah's cheeks colored. At six A.M., climbing out of a ship's galley wearing something she'd barely tossed on, with a man right behind her, she knew what they were thinking.

Summoning all her reserves of dignity, she turned to her host. "Thank you very much for the tour and the coffee," she said, ignoring the snickers from the dock.

Joe studied her slowly, barely concealing a grin.

"It wasn't much of a tour. I never showed you the bedroom."

"Some other time." She'd apologized, set things right, and now she was leaving. For good.

"Anytime, Miss Moran," he said, his voice like dark green felt, his smile like that of a satisfied cat.

Swiftly, she climbed down to the dock, her back to the three overgrown boys and the man whose low chuckle made the hairs rise on the back of her neck.

"Men!" she muttered. That summed it up completely.

Three

Susannah got a whiff of the coffee on her desk. "Thanks, Bill." The previous auditor's staff accountant may have had the most stilted handwriting she'd seen *and* the most idiosyncratic bookkeeping style, but when it came to coffee, he was a master.

"Coffee is accountant fuel, didn't you know that?"

"With rolls of adding machine paper for fiber," she said with a laugh, kicking a mile of serpentine tape out from under the desk.

As they settled down to work, Bill's comfortable baritone droned on about O&B circular 102, Bureau of Indian Affairs loan guarantees, and the ins and outs of reporting under the Indian Gambling Regulatory Act. As was often the way with the government, *why* the forms were necessary wasn't as important as when they were due.

"Tired?" he asked.

It was only lunchtime and figures swam before her eyes. But was she tired? "Not in the least," she answered, thinking it was amazing, considering she'd been getting up at dawn for the past two weeks. Half the time Joe's boat was gone by the time she awoke. Not that that had anything to do with her early hours, she told herself. Despite their proximity, she hadn't bumped into him at the marina again.

Bill set aside the printouts; his afternoon appointment allowed Susannah half a day off, or her version of one—carting a briefcase full of paperwork to her condo's breakfast nook which overlooked the bay.

She called good-bye to Bill and spent a few minutes deciding what to take home, her eyes drawn to the heavy-slatted blinds and the beckoning water beyond. There was something both peaceful and invigorating about living so close to the shore. That had to be the reason she'd been bounding out of bed every morning.

"Half the pay is the view of the bay," Joe intoned behind her.

Startled, she turned. "You're very good at that, sneaking up on people."

"Must be the Indian in me."

Susannah gave him a wry look. "I won't touch that one."

He leaned against the doorway, arms folded. The action emphasized the bulge in one bicep, the corded strength in a forearm. How he managed to look formal and remote in shorts and a knit top, Susannah couldn't fathom. Nor could she figure how he managed to send out the subterranean signals that made her feel as if some kind of radar were zeroing in on her. Perhaps it was his steady blue eyes.

Yes, he had a sense of humor, but at other times he seemed determined to keep her at a distance. "Why do I get the feeling you'd actually like it if I were prejudiced?"

Because he wanted her in his bed, Joe thought. It would be easier to resist if at least one of them objected to the idea. "Guess I've learned to be careful around palefaces."

Briefly, she wondered who'd taught him that caution. "I can work on the tan, but I won't promise anything but freckles."

That won a smile from him. "Am I interrupting your work?"

"Not at all. Please come in." In a way she was glad to see him. "I want to thank you for the other morning."

He shrugged. "Coffee was on me."

"I meant the boys on the dock."

"Did they bother you?"

"Just the idea that talk might get around."

He'd noticed her discomfort at the time. For someone with her usual poise, it seemed more than a momentary embarrassment. "If there'd been anything to talk about it, it would be strictly between us."

Silence settled in, both of them thinking how close they'd been to allowing something to happen, but neither wanting to acknowledge it.

"Thanks anyway. Rumors can do a lot of damage."

Joe recognized the sound of experience in her voice and wondered how, where, and when she'd been hurt by rumors. He filed it away for later, conveniently forgetting that he'd told himself on the way over that there would be no later, not in that sense. "I got a call today."

"On your boat?"

"On the answering machine at my apartment."

"Of course." Obviously he had to live somewhere. She'd always pictured him on the boat or in his tux at the casino. Not that she spent an inordinate amount of time imagining him anywhere.

Could she help it if he parked his charter right outside her door? "Guess you can't live at Manitou Lodge."

"You haven't been stopping by."

She hoped he meant by the casino. There was no way she was setting foot on his boat again. Just thinking of it made her feel crowded and breathless, the way she felt in this office with him backed up against the doorjamb like an unpredictable bear scratching its back against a tree.

"I can't gamble anymore." She paused to actually look at the stack of papers she'd been aimlessly sorting. With a frown she stuffed them all into her briefcase. "Not since we took on your accounting. That wouldn't be right." The click of briefcase latches underscored her words. Striding around the desk, she came within a few feet of him. He didn't back up as expected.

"I'll walk with you."

Even if he didn't know her well enough to read the look in her eyes, her hesitation was clear.

"Lead the way."

He watched her lock the office door. She was dressed simply but elegantly. The linen suit with its swaying full skirt wouldn't have stood out in Chicago the way it did in this cluttered back office. Here she looked like a million bucks.

Joe vowed to remember. She didn't belong, was passing through, and he was committed to his life here. Was it her fault that it was so empty? No matter how he tried filling up the hours, thoughts of Susannah Moran intruded. In her red dress, her boxer shorts, and too often, when he wasn't careful about screening his fantasies, in nothing at all.

"I'll show you a shortcut to the condos," he said gruffly, "an old Ottawa path." Even as they came out the back door to the parking lot, noonday heat rising from the asphalt, he wondered why he was prolonging this, why he didn't just give her the phone message and go home. "I used to follow this path as a kid, scouting around here in the summertime. It'll come out ten yards south of the condos."

"Guess we won't get lost with an honest-to-goodness native guide." At least she got half a smile out of him. She gave herself half a point. "Have you always lived here?" His background, and obvious mixed heritage, intrigued her.

"I lived downstate with my father, spending winters with him and summer vacations with my mother."

"Does she still live here?"

"Yes."

"She's Ottawa, then?"

"My father was a half breed." He didn't mention how quickly his father would deny any Native American background at all, how angry he'd be every summer when Joe came back darker than ever from playing outdoors, full of tribal stories and legends his mother told.

"I don't want any of that Indian garbage, you hear? When those boys play cowboys and Indians, you be the cowboy like anybody else! You hear me?" his father had insisted.

Joe still heard him. The questions that had confused him as a child remained. If his father hated the Ottawa part of his blood, why had he married Joe's mother? And how could he love his son, with his three quarter blood?

Maybe that's why Joe had taken so long to decide which world he really belonged in. Once he'd made the decision, he hadn't looked back. Until this woman had come along. She unsettled more than one part of him.

Susannah was looking at him curiously. She smiled when she caught his eye. "You got kind of quiet there."

With a scowl Joe reminded himself he wasn't there to share life stories. He had a message to give her. "About that phone call—"

Susannah stumbled and muttered a mild curse. "Could we hold on a minute, please?" The wooded path was a mix of trampled grass and packed sand. Her heels sank with every step. "Grass stains," she muttered, twisting her foot to show him.

Women's shoes, Joe pondered, staring at the high heels and the pale pink strap as delicate as the ankle it encased.

Putting out a hand to balance herself, she undid the straps. When she wobbled, Joe stepped closer. Looking down at her red hair, worn loose, he studied the way it fell forward across her shoulders, parting on either side of a neck that was bare, seashell white, and vulnerable. Would she jump if he planted a kiss there, a soft one? A lingering one? Would she run? Would he catch her in his arms, close enough for her breasts to brush his chest as they had on the boat?

The whine of a car passing on the road was the only sound, except for the birds, the pine needles parted by the wind above them, and the sound of his own breathing.

"Done!" She dangled the sandals by their flimsy straps. "Would you mind turning around for one more minute, please?"

When he hesitated, she made an imperious motion with her hand. "I'll explain."

He did as he was told, the rustling sounds behind him doing nothing to slow his heartbeat. Nor did the fact that she was barefoot and barelegged when he received permission to turn around.

Stuffing her nylons into her briefcase, she grinned at him. "Don't want to ruin these either."

No, but she'd just ruined any appetite he'd have for the next week. What did she have on under the flowing skirt now? A scrap of lace? Some silk?

They walked on in silence. The light was dappled and fresh, the floor of the small wood covered in ferns, dark green leaves, and small white flowers.

"What are these?" she asked.

"Trillium. They blossom in the spring, early summer."

"There's a restaurant around here named that."

"Yes, it's very fancy. You'd have to wear your red dress."

"Oh. Walking barefoot makes me feel light-years away from red dresses."

Joe noticed. The woman who was different every time he saw her was now a woodland sprite. He put his hand in the small of her back to help her over a fallen log.

"Any snakes around here?" she asked.

"None that would be lazy enough to let you step on them. It isn't that hot yet."

Although the air moved haphazardly through the trees, cooling as they neared the water, Susannah felt perspiration starting between her breasts. The dirt path remained cool beneath her feet. "I'll have to walk in the bay to wash these off." She wiggled her toes.

Joe looked carefully down at them. Then slowly back up. He imagined her skirt up around her knees, around her thighs, as she waded in the water. Vividly, he imagined her on a bed of moss, the skirt around her waist this time, his hand on her breast. When his gaze reached her face, her eyes were wide and filled with caution.

"Joe?"

He couldn't concentrate on anything but that breathy voice, the pale, creamy skin brightened with patches of color from the walk, the heat. He had to do something or else he'd be taking her in his arms. "There's a great view at the top of that hill. Come on."

Taking off at a brisk pace, he didn't give her much choice but to follow. The man acted as if he had something to work off. Susannah swallowed and wished they had a canteen. Initially watching her step, she put one foot in front of the other on the leaf-littered path, her carefree mood fading as the path narrowed.

"Poison ivy," Joe said without turning, adding a throw away gesture toward a group of ferns.

She scampered closer behind him.

Either the hill was steeper than it looked, or she was out of shape. The temperature was definitely rising. She surreptitiously wiped a trickle of sweat from beneath her breast through her blouse.

That's when he turned, his eyes catching the spot of dampness. "Still with me?"

For now she answered silently. With a wry grin that was strictly for his benefit, she waved the briefcase. "Not fair, I'm carrying something."

"Set it somewhere."

She leaned it against a boulder.

Joe clutched a young sapling and scaled the crest of the hill. "Up here," he said, watching her keenly.

He didn't move. She had to come to him. She swallowed, took a few slow breaths, and met him there.

"It is wonderful," she said. A hundred feet above the water they gazed out at the peninsula dotted with cherry orchards set in patterns on the hills across the way. The bay glistened below, the sound of waves a low rhythmic splash. "The water's so clear you can see the stones sparkling from up here. It's beautiful."

Joe nodded, never taking his eyes off her. Her hair glittered in the sunlight, wisps blowing back with the breeze, strands clinging to the perspiration on her neck. He'd wanted to show her this—the place he'd come to as a child, a teenager, a man alone—to show and share it with someone who could appreciate how beautiful and how sacred it was to him. Someone who could make it complete by coming into his arms.

The light flickered through the leaves and the air grew hot. He'd told himself all along he didn't want to kiss her, then she turned. He willed her eyes to close, her lips to part. One arm slowly pulled her flat against him as he pressed his mouth to hers.

When he was finished with the first kiss, he drew back, his breath ragged and harsh. "Don't you want to argue?"

"Argue?" Susannah repeated with vague wonder. Nothing had ever felt so right. She was shy about lifting her arms to his neck, for she knew the motion made her breasts rise. She felt his chest quiver, the arm at her back tighten. She measured the width of his shoulders with her palms. Without her shoes she was shorter; she had to tilt her head back.

"I—I shouldn't want this. I just got over—" A bad relationship. She didn't say it, didn't want it to intrude. She looked away at the glittering water. She'd wanted to use this summer to relax, to put past mistakes behind her. But some things had no doubts attached. Not when they felt so right. She took a deep breath and looked into eyes as clear and blue as the water. "I shouldn't want this," she said, her voice firm and low, "but I do."

She didn't hesitate this time to touch his neck, his hair. He raked her lips with his own, his tongue thrusting into her mouth.

It took a moment for the giggles to distract them. All she knew was that he'd torn his mouth away. Staring into the shadowy forest, her eyes focused on four chattering elves scampering into the trees at the bottom of the hill. Leprechauns, she wondered dazedly. Native American children, she realized, and they were carrying something. "My briefcase!"

Joe gave chase first, muttering oaths all the way. Barefoot, Susannah reached the hamlet a few minutes behind him, convinced she'd stepped on every pointed twig in Leelanau County.

In the middle of a clearing, hands on his hips, Joe stood rock still and made an announcement. "If that briefcase isn't returned immediately, you're all deer bait!"

A giggle straight out of Munchkinland made Susannah cover her mouth to hide a smile.

While Joe stalked in the direction of some rustling bushes, Susannah took stock of the clearing.

There were four trailers. Hitches still testified to their past mobility, as did wheels lifted off the ground by cinder blocks. One had a fenced enclosure scattered with toys, another a pickup truck parked nearby. There were numerous sheds and outbuildings, and in the middle of it all something that looked like an ice-fishing shanty with a chimney attached, smoke drifting upward. Did people live here year-round? And who'd heat an outhouse in June?

Joe sneaked around the side of a slapdash shed

made of scrap wood. His plan was immediately apparent and effective. He'd flush them out while Susannah stood by to nab them. She caught one, a small boy, by the scruff of the neck.

"All right, where's my briefcase," she ordered in her best military tone. Having a first sergeant for a father occasionally came in handy.

The boy mumbled something, tugging at the bottom of his striped shirt.

"Was that Ottawa or Ojibway?" Susannah asked Joe sweetly through gritted teeth.

"I couldn't make it out." With his palm flat on the child's head, Joe turned the boy's attention his way, asking a question in Ottawa. The boy made a short reply. Joe gave him another command, and the youngster ran off. "I think it's in there," he motioned. "I'll get it out before it's ruined."

The outhouse? Susannah moaned. She could hardly imagine the damage to her papers if they'd tossed it in there. "You aren't just going in, are you? Someone might be in there."

Joe yanked open the door. Smoke wafted out into the compound. Susannah peered over his shoulder. "Were they sneaking cigars in here?"

"It's not that kind of smoke. This is for fish."

As her eyes adjusted to the gloom, she made out rows of dead fish. Her heart sank as she remembered the hand-lettered Smoked Fish signs dotting the highway on her way there. Gingerly, she took the briefcase from Joe. "It isn't going to smell like this forever, is it?"

He chuckled, and soon they were both laughing. It didn't stop Susannah from noticing the way the lines crinkled around his eyes, the white teeth against his dark skin, the mouth she'd tasted moments before.

It was hard to convince herself the kiss had been wrong despite her insistence that it had to end there. It unlocked a need in both of them, one she suspected neither of them had openly acknowledged. Lonely, searching, they'd found each other. There was something amazing and fortuitous in that. They'd gotten off to such a bad start, each pretending to be someone else. Even now they were so different. But they fit.

Susannah shook her head forcefully. It was just one of those things. For a blistering moment everything felt exactly right. And that's about how long that kind of relationship lasted. Better not make a big deal about it, she decided. Friendship was fine, but she was there on business.

Remembering her business, she noticed a latch on her briefcase was unsnapped. "This whole thing could've popped open. I'd better check inside—" Before she could undo the other latch, a second boy came whooping through the clearing, a pair of panty hose trailing from his upraised arm like a flag.

"Oh, no!" Susannah wailed.

"Hold it!" Joe yelled.

Looking over his shoulder at his pursuers, the little boy didn't see the plump, square-set woman who'd emerged from one of the trailers. "Here now," she said, grasping him by both arms before he crashed into her. "Where are you going with those? And where you going to wear them to, eh? Think these'd look good on you?"

Chagrined at the teasing, the boy gave her a rebellious but quickly tamed look.

"You going to apologize to this lady?"

"Yes, Miss Mona."

"Say it to her, then."

He mumbled something in his own language as Susannah came over.

"He don't know your name," the older woman smiled.

"Susannah. Susannah Moran." She wasn't quite sure whom to shake hands with first, so she extended her hand to the boy. "You may call me Miss Moran."

Mona returned the panty hose to him and he gave them to Susannah. "Sorry, Miss Moran," he said to the grass.

Mustering as much dignity as a general accepting a sword of surrender, Susannah thanked him. It wasn't easy, not when she caught the glimmer of laughter in the older woman's eyes.

Released, the boy raced off. That left Susannah standing with a handful of panty hose, Joe keeping well back. She caught the woman eyeing him. "It's a long story," Susannah began.

"I know that much," Mona said with a short laugh, giving her a quick perusal. "Come on in."

Expecting Joe to follow, Susannah entered the trailer. Inside it was cramped but clean, cluttered with a variety of crafts, quill boxes, and basket weavings.

"Do you make these? They're beautiful."

"Thank you."

"And these dyed strips?"

"That is a traditional Ottawa design long associated with *Nish Nah Be.*"

"*Nish—*?"

"*Nah Be.* It means people. Us."

"It's marvelous." Not sure of the etiquette for this situation, Susannah floundered. She was normally good with people. She cleared her throat, aware she was being evaluated in Mona's polite but offhand way. "Do you sell these?" she asked.

Mona pulled herself up to her fullest height, all of five feet, and let out a rumbling, welcoming laugh. "Of course. You think I need these all for myself? It makes me good money. Besides, I'm good at it."

Susannah felt instantly at home. "All right, then, how many may I buy?"

Joe stood in the clearing, as still as a deer. He looked around him the way he'd looked every summer when he'd come back. The trailers were rusty. The yards were mostly weeds and wildflowers. The hinges on Mona's screen door creaked. The sound of it banging shut still hovered in the air with the sound of crickets and cicadas. The road leading out of there was nothing but a two-track through the woods. Susannah would never have stumbled upon it, not if he hadn't brought her there.

What would she think? The boys had been dirty. Sure they were boys, out of school for the summer and getting into mischief. But he wanted them clean, hair combed for her. Otherwise, she'd see exactly what he saw when he looked around him. Poverty. Slapped-together shacks. Rust and weeds in a clearing in the woods.

Angrily, he told himself he hadn't come back to live up to someone else's standards. And yet . . .

The worn pickup truck was parked because its owner had no work. The smoked fish and arts and crafts brought in a little extra money. Yes, the casino pulled in a lot of cash, and there was a section of tract housing going up a couple miles away. But real economic progress was slow. Susannah had seen the prosperous side at the lodge. Then Joe had led her here. Part of him knew there was no better way to show her how different their worlds were. Part of him cursed.

The screen door screeched open. Susannah

stepped carefully down the metal stairs, arms full of baskets. "I'll send over a traveler's check. What is your last name?"

"You couldn't pronounce it, honey, much less spell it. Just put Mona on it. You can even send it with Joe. I should be seeing him sometime," she added, her eyes intent and curious as he turned their way.

Susannah's briefcase in one hand, Joe approached and greeted the woman in Ottawa. She replied. "Ready to go?" he said to Susannah.

"Guess so."

With a quick good-bye to Mona, Susannah followed Joe through a barely discernible break in the trees. "Did I say something wrong?"

He kept walking ahead of her. Susannah trotted up beside him. "Sorry, but I don't believe in women following three paces behind their men."

Their men. She immediately regretted the familiarity behind that. Just because they'd kissed . . . "Joe, would you be so kind as to tell me what's bothering you?"

"You didn't see it?"

"See what?"

"That. The village."

"What about it?"

"Aren't you going to say something about the poor Indians? The poor, destitute Native Americans?"

She stopped, mouth agape. "I realize jobs are needed, some self-help opportunities—"

"I take it you have the answers? Old-fashioned liberal do-goodism?"

Why was he turning on her? A swelling anger blinded her to nostalgia over something as meager as a kiss. "Hold on here just a minute. When have I ever been that patronizing?"

His voice was harsh, his question contemptuous. "Then why did you buy these?"

She glanced down at her purchases. Cheeks flushed, she stood her ground. "I bought them because they're beautiful and very well made."

"Buying some friends? Ingratiating yourself with the natives? Trading traveler's checks instead of beads?"

She made a conscious effort to lower her voice as it rose in anger. "I wanted something to decorate my condo with. Since my family never lived anyplace for long, I have this habit of making wherever I live home."

"Home," he said flatly.

It was true. Although her job provided little chance to stop moving, she'd always had a deep-seated sentimental notion about having a real home, a husband, a family. His doubtful look almost spurred her into telling him so.

"You want a home? Well, you've just seen mine."

She stopped at the edge of the road, traffic zipping by them. "That's where you live?"

"No, but my mother does. You just met her."

Four

Guiding her across the busy road, he took her arm so roughly, she had to grasp the baskets close to her chest.

"Why didn't you introduce us?"

"I didn't see any need."

Susannah ripped her arm out of his grip. "Joe, will you tell me why you're so angry? What did I do wrong?"

She'd kissed him, made him feel a firestorm of emotions he wanted suppressed—until the right woman came along, preferably an Ottawa. But it was hardly something he could explain to a woman he'd been kissing not half an hour before.

He took the pile of baskets, and they began walking slowly through the parking lot to her condo at the end of the development.

"Are you ashamed?" she asked carefully.

Of a lot of things, he thought. Of his own inability to fight this attraction, to keep his hands off her. And of what that said about him and the promise he'd made to himself three years earlier. He was supposed to be dedicated to his people and their welfare. "It's one of the worse sections on the reservation. That old trailer shakes every time the wind blows."

Mona's place, his mother's. Susannah thought of the nondescript suburban housing her parents called home. They'd traveled for so many years, yet when they retired it had been to a brand new subdivision that couldn't look more like an army base. "Wouldn't it be nice if we could buy our parents the kind of homes they deserve?" she wondered aloud.

"I tried. She wouldn't accept it." He cursed softly but eloquently. His offer to buy her a house wasn't something he revealed to many people. Nor her refusal.

Susannah understood. "It's hard to offer something and be turned down."

The observation hung in the air. He pursed his lips but didn't reply.

"I liked her," she said simply.

Joe stopped opposite her patio door and looked at her. There were faint freckles under her peachy skin. Her gaze was honest, open, her emotions genuine. She wouldn't hesitate befriending a woman she'd just met, a woman from a different culture, different social strata, by enthusiastically buying up an armload of crafts.

She wouldn't hesitate to open up to him if he let her.

She set her things on the picnic table and leaned lightly on the sliding glass doors. He could see the reflection of her hair, and his hand reaching toward it. A decorative brick wall separated them from the other units—a little privacy.

She looked surprised when he touched her and moved in closer, cupping the back of her head in his hand. Her lips parted, and she started to say something. He shook his head. He didn't want arguments, he didn't want consent. He wanted to know why he was so drawn to a woman he couldn't have. "This won't work. Not for the two of us."

"Are the differences that great? We could talk."

"And say what?" Just the memory of her running her hands through his hair on the hill was enough to make his heart rate skyrocket. "We could talk until the sun set, and I'd still be a fool to want this." His voice was rough, a harsh whisper. "Put your hands on me."

She complied, palms on his chest, sensing the inferno of heat radiating from him. At her back, the coolness of the glass penetrated her clothes. *He* was grappling with a tangle of questions, not her. There was no how or why for her, she simply knew she wanted this every bit as much as he did. The reasons would come later, after his mouth had finished with hers.

Their lips met, mouths dueling. She heard a sound rumble out of her throat. A bubble of laughter, deep and uninhibited. Tension released so a new tension could build. He didn't have to tell her that sound could drive a man over the edge, she felt it in the jerk of his body, the way his tongue plundered deeper, marauding, invading.

Her nails dug crescents in his arms when the need to pull him close grew stronger. Her hands found his neck, and she twisted her head to the side. Teeth clicked and collided, no time for apologies. She'd never reacted so completely to a man. The emotion was frightening, suffocating. She wanted it so badly she could taste it.

A boat horn in the marina sounded, and they broke the kiss. Joe's eyes bored into hers as he blocked her against the glass with his body, his chest heaving. Whatever passion he'd aroused in her still fired her dark eyes. The depth to which he'd entered her with his tongue seemed to sound in the husky whisper of her voice.

"Joe."

"Do you trust me?"

She nodded. In his arms, she trusted him implicitly, a man of unshakable integrity, bold, on fire. "Maybe we should slow down, take this a step at a time."

Time to think wasn't what he wanted. It might be what he needed.

"Maybe we should call it off completely," Joe said.

All he saw were barriers. And a just-kissed mouth curving into a smile that sweetly disagreed with him.

"We'll talk," she said.

It would take an effort on his part to put them back on the cagey, distant terms they'd been on in her office. "On the boat?"

She studied *The Sporting Chance*. "Alone might be too tempting. Sometime when our hormones won't be in danger of getting carried away." She couldn't resist running her hand down one perfect bicep. "Like adults, you know?"

He swallowed. Hard. "On the boat." Since when was his voice so gravelly? "We won't be alone. That phone call I mentioned earlier was from someone in your Chicago office. A secretary called about a charter for Saturday. Says you're expected to attend. Said her boss wanted it for the day."

"Who?"

"Said you know him. Didn't say more."

Her face drained of all color. She suspected Keith, and he was the last person she wanted around. The glass against her hot skin was no longer cooling, it was clammy. Seduced by the rightness of being in Joe's arms, she didn't want to remember how dreadfully wrong her judgment about men could be.

"Would you mind if I canceled the whole thing? Do you need the business?" It was as tactful as she could make it.

Obviously the money didn't bother him, but his eyes were wary and alert. "If it's not confirmed by Friday, I'll open it up for any takers."

"I'll give him a call."

She slid the door back to go inside, swiping the armload of baskets off the picnic table. He'd set her briefcase by the wall. She picked it up.

"Susannah?"

"What?"

"You said something about talking. Like you're not doing right now."

He was good at subtle interrogation. How had she forgotten that? "There's no reason for anyone from the office to make the trip, that's all."

"Is it the man who taught you to be careful about rumors?" Quick and intuitive and right. Joe knew as soon as he saw the flash of anger in her eyes.

She imagined the stories racing across the reservation. "You've heard about this?" she asked sharply.

"Not a whisper. But I wouldn't mind hearing it from you."

She shrugged but couldn't manage the carefree look to go with it. "A disaster, okay? An office disaster, a rather public affair. A secret that was painfully obvious to everyone but the woman involved. Get the picture?"

He did. The fact that she wouldn't look him directly in the eye told him even more. He wasn't sure how she'd take the rest of the message. "The secretary said he was bringing his wife."

Wife? That was a new one. A girlfriend to share his hotel room was more like it. Keith wasn't without a bedmate for long. Susannah worried her lip with her teeth. "Consider it canceled."

Susannah slid the glass door shut with a whoosh, wishing the damn thing slammed. She was in the mood for a tantrum.

Keith! Why was he coming? To cause trouble? To stare over her shoulder at the new account? To see if he could still push all the right buttons? She didn't need that kind of interference.

She spread the baskets on the kitchen counter with a hollow bump. Of course, railing against all the wrongs Keith had done her might keep her mind off Joe Bond for all of fifteen minutes. So might laying out her accounting paper, plugging in her adding machine, changing into shorts and a top, and getting to work.

Fifteen minutes later, staring at the green zeros on her adding machine, she went still inside. Thinking of Joe's kiss could do that to her—thinking about the tenderness of his kiss on the hill, the harder, more blatant need of this last kiss. So raw. Like her response . . .

A gull landed on the patio and squawked at her. She'd forgotten to set out toast crusts that morning.

"No goodies today," she called.

Her beady-eyed friend gave her a baleful look and flew off. Susannah glanced blankly at the papers on the table in front of her, realizing only then that her fingertips still rested on her lips.

She looked out at Joe's boat. What were they

going to do, the two of them? One moment she was willing to take any risk, to try again, to always be open to new people, new chances. The next moment, if history was any example, she was packing and leaving for another assignment. She was a nester, yes, but the migratory kind. A home and a steady relationship wasn't for her. She'd tried. She'd failed. When she'd arrived there, she'd been resigned to a life of moving on. Or so she thought.

Scanning the water and the other bobbing boats, sails already dotting the bay, she knew with utter certainty that she loved this place as it was, as she was. She told herself she didn't need that dream of a home and someone to share it with.

Joe had no one to share this with either. She wondered at his sudden bouts of abrasiveness and withdrawal. She wanted to air their differences, help him with whatever he was struggling against.

"Uh-oh. The earth mother/redeemer strikes again. It is not your responsibility to make things easier for a man. Got that?" She told herself.

Keith had left her holding the bag, and taking the blame alone. She'd learned the hard way.

"Thanks, Keith," she ground out through gritted teeth. The phone was already in her hand, the line ringing.

"Whitman, Jablonski, and Parritt. How may I help you?"

"Keith Sanderson, please."

Before getting any more deeply involved with Joe, she needed this reminder about her own nurturing nature and the mistakes unrealistic dreams led to.

"Sanderson here."

"Keith," she said flatly.

"Susannah! Darling, how are you?" He was as effusive and charming and transparent as ever.

"I don't want you coming up this weekend, Keith."

"Oh." A short pause. "And if I wanted to?"

In Keith's world that was all the justification one needed.

"Everything's under control here, Keith. This isn't your section, and even if it were, there's hardly been time to put procedures in place." She waited out Keith's silence, fighting the sinking feeling that she'd shot all her ammunition at once.

She wasn't sure if she imagined it or if she could actually hear his pencil ticking against the edge of his desk like a drumstick.

"As I recall," he drawled, "there was talk at the staff meeting about someone taking a ride up there."

"I don't really need someone looking over my shoulder. Jack wouldn't have given me the assignment if he hadn't thought I was perfectly capable."

"It was Jack who was talking about heading up there. Said it's very pretty, if a bit of a small town."

She'd jumped to the wrong conclusion. Susannah bit back a curse, realizing the only bright spot was that Keith couldn't see her flushing cheeks. "That's one of the reasons I came."

"Really?" He asked it as if no one willingly stepped out of the fast lane. "Any others?"

"To put some distance between us, frankly."

"Sounds prudent. Although I am flattered you thought of me when you called. Want me to transfer you to Jack so you can warn him off?"

"No." Susannah rubbed her eyes. "I'm not warning anyone off." She heard the extension beeping in Keith's office. "Sorry about the mis-understanding, Keith. I'll let you answer that."

"No problem, darling. It's always interesting to hear from you. Sometimes it's downright intriguing."

Joe reported to the casino.

He poked his head in William's empty office and scrawled a message that he'd decided to work the casino that night.

At least from there he couldn't stare at her condo. That didn't keep him from imagining himself chafing in his tux. He couldn't walk in the door anymore without his eyes going to the craps table in search of the woman in that bright red dress.

He cursed as he left the office.

"Something wrong, Joe?" One of the blackjack dealers strolled by, grinning at Joe's obvious black mood.

Joe cursed again and headed for his apartment to change. In a way, he hoped there'd be trouble later. He'd enjoy playing bouncer, tossing a couple drunks out the door, fighting something easier than thoughts of Susannah Moran and her high spirits, Susannah and her lusciously curving mouth, Susannah and his mother, chatting on the rickety stairs of the trailer.

He stopped in the middle of the parking lot. Is that why he was ready to bite the top off a beer bottle? Was he a thirty-six-year-old man worrying what his mother thought of his taste in women?

Yes and no.

It was true he valued Mona's opinion and her wisdom. But mostly he was concerned with promises he'd made.

"Damn it to hell," he spat out, "I never promised to become a monk!"

The three of them came around the corner of the condo, still greeting each other, smiling and exchanging kisses. On board, Joe straightened and watched as they crossed the beach to where the dock began. Even from a distance Susannah's smile beamed. Recognizing the staff member who'd charted the boat, Joe noted that Jack was as fatherly and friendly as he'd been at the council meeting. A petite, dark-haired woman was with them—Jack's wife.

Joe climbed the ladder with the last of the fishing gear, getting things in order on board. That didn't stop him from glancing up as their steps sounded on the wooden planking.

Jack's prematurely white hair topped a ruddy complexion on a boyish face. It was easy to picture him at prep school, an Ivy League college.

Joe had never pictured Susannah as Ivy League. She didn't have that born-to-it polish her senior partner had. He suspected she had the determination, the desire to get ahead in the world he'd ditched long before.

Every year businessmen like him realized there was more to life than a career. That didn't mean there weren't plenty of people to take their places. Joe had never kidded himself that he was indispensable. Corporations groomed talent like Susannah's. As long as she was willing to fit the mold.

He remembered the way she fit against him—as if they were made for each other, made to be together. His fist tightened around a fishing pole.

"We need to talk," she'd said. But she hadn't

called or come by. She could have walked down this dock any morning, met him on *The Sporting Chance.* He doubted they would have gotten much talking done, though.

He reminded himself it had been only four days. Four days during which he'd been tied in knots.

A few words wafted up to him as the three of them walked down the dock. He had a few minutes to force himself to remember this was strictly a business charter. And Susannah was a business-woman. That's what brought her there. That's what would take her away. He knew the type. You could say he was an expert.

Five

"—Our expert," Susannah said, indicating Joe with a wave of her arm. "He knows everything there is about fishing, sailing, and navigating on the Great Lakes."

"Hardly," Joe muttered, swinging down the ladder to greet his guests. "But I can promise you a safe and enjoyable afternoon."

Which was more than he was in for himself. One look at Susannah, and it was all he could do not to reach out to her.

So he did just that. "May I give you a hand getting up the ladder?"

His palm was warm on the small of her back. At his touch a dozen lights seemed to flicker over her skin, like the morning sunlight sparkling on the water. Susannah had to remind herself to take a breath before she spoke.

"Let me introduce you to Jack and Machiko first."

"Sure."

He withdrew his hand instantly. Susannah missed it being there. It felt right. She had a silly idea they should be holding hands, like the couple opposite them.

"This is Jack Hainford, I'm sure you remember him from the council meeting. And Jack, you remember Joe Bond."

"How could I forget," Jack laughed heartily, shaking hands. "Never met a man foolish enough to turn down a bribe like that."

"I don't usually suggest it," Susannah added quickly.

"Next time she offers I'll know better." Joe's quick look wasn't lost on Susannah. Next time they'd be playing for more than chips, throwing caution away instead of dice.

Susannah introduced Joe to Jack's Japanese wife, Machiko.

"Nice to meet you."

"I can understand why you've become so attached to this place so quickly, Susannah," Machiko said.

Had she, Joe wondered. Was it the place or him? Or just another rung on the ladder?

"Does it show?" Susannah asked.

"Jack says your reports glow."

Jack rolled his eyes heavenward. "The way this woman reads into things. We're looking forward to seeing reality from the water, Joe."

"Let's climb aboard, then."

Jack handed his wife up, which was no easy task with the hefty beach bag she carried on her arm. Susannah followed, then Jack, giving Joe a moment to loosen the ropes on the pylons and get his thoughts under control.

He was as coiled as the ropes. Susannah seemed perfectly at ease. She wore matching shorts and sweater, perfect for a business outing. It wasn't her fault he couldn't keep his eyes off her. She was as proper and businesslike as L. L. Bean could make her.

The way the shorts accentuated her legs was strictly his problem.

Their gear stashed and deck chairs set out, Joe climbed the fixed ladder to the bridge four rungs above the aft deck. He took a few minutes to chart their course.

While Jack and Machiko settled in, Susannah made sure her deck chair had its back to the bridge.

"What kind of equipment you think he's got up there?" Jack asked. "From here it looks like an airplane instrument panel."

Susannah would not be goaded into craning her neck. Jack had caught her glancing up at Joe at least three times in the last five minutes. She knew what the instrument panel looked like. She had every detail of the bridge memorized.

A captain's chair was bolted onto the floor by the wheel. The bank of dials and gauges was complemented on either side by a couple of mounted screens. Joe stood beneath a removable blue awning, behind a clear plastic windshield that blocked the wind.

"You seem to trust our captain," Jack noted.

"Completely." She crossed her legs. Trust and relaxation were the emotions to convey here, with a touch of easy confidence. But that was easier said than done with Joe around and her emotions in turmoil.

Certainly she trusted him. She just wasn't sure she knew him. One moment he looked at her as intensely as any lover, the next he was all business. As for her, daydreams about holding hands had no place on her agenda. Whatever the reason Jack and Machiko had come, she wanted to show she was capable, cool, and could handle whatever work came her way. She wanted out from under the scandals and mistakes. She wasn't there to give her heart another going over.

Unfortunately, putting all her energies into her work these last few days hadn't had any affect on her dreams. She'd missed Joe. She wanted to talk to him. But she couldn't, not with Jack's friendly and astute eyes picking up her every move.

Joe climbed down from the bridge. He walked around the edge of the cabin and cast off the last rope, his deck shoes squeaking like Susannah's nerves.

"Need help?" Jack offered before Susannah could.

"I've got it. Your only job is to relax and enjoy. We'll be under way in a few minutes."

Susannah watched Joe's back muscles work under a white knit shirt as he reeled in the rope, his arms glistening, his legs muscled and sturdy under the many-pocketed tan shorts. Each pocket was buttoned down, like the looks he sent her way.

"Care for a mint?" Machiko was no less an observer than Jack. Having found a roll of wintergreen breath mints in that voluminous bag, her polite offer interrupted yet more of Susannah's stargazing.

"No, thank you." Susannah stuck her hand into the big cooler. The ice was chunky and stiff. She tugged one can free, examining the label. "Is it too early in the morning for a beer?"

"Not if you toss me one," Jack replied.

She helped herself to a root beer. Machiko chose lemon lime. For some reason she couldn't fathom, Susannah was parched. Her lips seemed in constant need of moistening.

Joe climbed to the bridge again. Susannah told herself she would not look. The engines roared then grumbled beneath them, churning up white waves and a slick of gasoline that rainbow-stained the water behind their slip. They passed the harbor master and headed out into the bay.

"Wave good-bye to the shoreline," Jack said.

She and Machiko dutifully waved.

"When do you think we'll stop for painting?" Machiko asked.

"Painting?"

She had her watercolors set up already. "I'd like to paint an island, the water, some pines."

"Don't forget the fishing," Jack said.

As if they weren't already, Susannah thought.

"I suppose I could go ask," Jack muttered doubtfully, squinting up at the bridge as if it were as high as a lighthouse and more difficult to climb.

"Would you like me to?" The offer was made before Susannah had a chance to think through the consequences. Both Jack's and Machiko's faces lit right up.

"Why don't you, dear?"

"Good idea, Susie. You know the fellow."

Susannah rose slowly, wondering how exactly they'd maneuvered her into this one. She'd forgotten what a formidable team Jack and Machiko could be. "I'll be right back."

"Take your time, dear. I'm sure the islands will wait."

She climbed the ladder to the bridge. Joe cast a glance over his shoulder as she stepped up beside him. He swiveled in the captain's chair to adjust a screen.

"What is that?" she asked.

"Depth finder."

Susannah looked around and sighed. Wasn't that what one did when confronted with nature's beauty? The view was marvelous and eased some of her tension—but not for long. Restlessly, she asked after each piece of equipment, learning and forgetting the names as he rattled them off.

"Is that why you came up here, Susannah?"

"Not entirely." She'd wanted to escape her guests' scrutiny. Instead, she was busy watching the muscles in his legs bunch as he shifted his weight on the edge of the chair.

Balancing, her hand went to the upholstered back of the chair when they hit a wave. Joe sat back, her thumb grazing his shirt. She withdrew it. Below, Machiko was lowering her eyes and smiling at Jack in a thoroughly knowing way.

"You said you didn't think you'd visit my boat again." Joe's eyes crinkled. Was it a smile or a squint, she wondered. She couldn't tell.

"Women do change their minds, you know."

"Especially when duty calls." When business dictated, a true career woman would even change her lover. Joe knew that from experience. Maybe it was better they weren't lovers. Maybe he'd better forget she was standing there, her legs close enough to brush his when *The Sporting Chance* hit a wash from a passing boat and rolled lightly to the left.

But first he had to do something about that mane of hair lashing her lightly freckled face.

Susannah felt a hand clamp down on her head. "What?" Caught daydreaming again.

"I said you need this," Joe repeated, dropping a

shapeless fisherman's cap on her hair. "You're going to get windburn."

Susannah whipped it off, noting with a grimace the fly-fishing lures used for adornment, the wrinkled narrow cloth brim. She tossed it on the console. "Never."

"While you're out in the sun, you'll wear it. I don't want anyone getting sunstroke."

His gruff order and veiled concern only made her smile. "Anyone ever tell you you're a real dictator when you get some power?"

"I have been told I come on strong." He smiled, that tempting devilish glint in his eye. There was a dare there, and a guarded kind of reserve.

She'd seen the power he tried to rein in. Sensed it. Been rendered breathless in the arms of it. She didn't mind tempting it. "Are you telling me you're ruthless?"

"I've scared away a few women in my time." And watched one walk away.

"Should I ask how or why?"

"I stare. It's considered rude in our culture. Having been raised in the white world, I didn't realize until I came back."

Susannah pondered that for a moment. There were so many unspoken rules between cultures. How had Machiko and Jack overcome their differences? Could she and Joe?

He was looking calmly, unflinchingly, into her eyes. Making a point. An involuntary shudder raced up Susannah's spine as he studied her. "Why is it rude?"

"It shows you doubt what someone is saying. Of course, it's just the opposite in the white world. There people look you in the eye to establish trust. That's why we can be seen as shy or shifty. We

don't make eye contact the way a good job appli-
cant should."

She chuckled and pondered his blue eyes. "No
one would ever mistake you for shifty. Or shy."

"I live here now, not there," he reminded her
gruffly. Here he was too pushy, moved too fast,
would revert to his white ways sooner or later. At
least, that's what people said. He handed her the
hat. "You're too pale to sit in the sun."

"Calling me a paleface?"

"If the hat fits . . ."

Susannah replied with a mock whine. "It'll ruin
my hair."

He grinned slowly, like the pace of his words.
"Even if your hair were spread all over a pillow
with my hands tangled in it all night, it'd be fine
with me."

His cool blue eyes held hers. Messages passed
between them. He was right, she thought with a
swallow, he did come on strong.

"Besides, you'll fry your brain, *squandeh*. Unless you want to hide up here in the shade with
me."

"Sorry, Cap'n, can't hide."

"Business calls?"

He saw her careful glance toward Jack and
Machiko. Tugging the hat out of her hands, Joe
stuffed it back on her head. A thunk of his broad
palm anchored it there for emphasis. He was laying
claim for all to see. The woman was his unless
she said otherwise. Better to know now if she was
going to refuse him.

The significance seemed lost on Susannah. She
adjusted the depth finder to serve as a mirror.
Angling the hat from one tilt to another, she finally pulled it down over her forehead, smiling at

him like some freckled urchin he'd picked up dock-side. "What's *squandeh* mean, anyway?"

"Red."

"That's me?"

"That's what you're going to be if you don't stay out of the sun."

"And what are you?"

I'm the man who wants you, he almost said.

Jack's voice sounded from the rungs below. "Permission to ascend?"

"Come on up," Joe called, his eyes never leaving Susannah's. She had to tear her gaze away from his as Jack joined them.

Joe gave Jack a quick glance. As Susannah's superior, he could be Joe's biggest rival. It didn't help that the man was likable. And no fool.

"What kind of hardware you got up here?"

"The lady was just asking me that."

It could have been a double entendre, but Joe kept his voice carefully flat, making it more of an alibi. "As I was explaining to Susannah, this is Lorcan, this is the depth finder, these are oil and gas gauges. As you can see, we're approaching a deepwater point. We may even pick up a school of fish on the screen."

He slowed the engines. "We can all go down on deck in a minute, and I'll divide up the fishing gear."

On deck they went through the rules, the catch limits, the kinds of bait.

"Will you be joining us, Mrs. Hainford?"

Machiko shuddered and demurred. "I prefer creating from water, not taking from it." She held up a sheet of drawing pads. "Will we be passing any islands, Mr. Bond?"

Blushing, Susannah wondered how she'd guessed

that neither Susannah nor her husband had remembered to ask.

"With a few trees and some rocky shores perhaps?"

"I think I can oblige," Joe answered. "If you two don't mind trolling."

"Not at all."

Joe restarted the engine and they sailed northward until a small island came into sight off the starboard side. "Will this do?"

"Excellent, Mr. Bond."

He was very good with people, Susannah noted —on board the charter, at the casino, no doubt in his former life as well. She sensed he'd shared only the stresses with her, the disappointments, the frustrations of not being able to move at his own speed. That was trust too.

But there were things holding both of them back, she reminded herself as she watched him drop anchor. He wasn't the only one with obligations.

"Like it here, Susannah?"

"So far, Jack. It's a beautiful area."

"Everything is good-looking," Machiko said with a smile. "Quite striking." She set up her easel on the gently rocking deck.

Susannah concentrated on baiting her hook. Her voice was low and meant only for Jack as they cast their lines and leaned against the rail. "Speaking of bait, why are you two here?"

Jack raised a brow. "We wanted to visit you, Susie."

"You had me over for dinner before I left. Don't tell me a month has made me irresistible." She could be as flippant and easy going as Jack, but the issue was real. "Are you checking up on me? Does this have anything to do with Keith?"

"Speaking of worms."

"I'm serious. Is my work in doubt?"

"No. But it's obviously done you good to get out of Chicago."

Was he suggesting she get out permanently? No. Caught between Jack's subtle probing and Joe's silent demands, she was getting paranoid. She pulled off the silly cap and reeled in her line. Not a nibble.

"I want to do a good job, Jack. That's always been important to me."

"Nobody doubts you can."

"Don't they?"

Jack ducked her gaze and looked out at the blue water. "You were brought in too late to have made the worst of the Showcase errors. Give me credit for figuring that one out. Those errors were built in from conception. I think we all know where the blame lies."

"That doesn't mean I didn't make some pretty fundamental mistakes."

"No one is entirely innocent, I suppose. Taking responsibility for one's actions is a sign of maturity."

"So why was Keith promoted and I shipped out?"

Jack was using his look-at-the-big-picture voice. "There is a reason behind this. You should see this account as an opportunity."

"It's a breather, anyway." The day would come when she'd have to go back to the main office. What then? "I won't make you sorry you sent me."

He winked and put an arm around her shoulders. "I'm not, Susie. Down the road, I hope I can say I was the one who started this whole thing, one way or the other."

Wondering what he meant by that, her thoughts wandered and her line became hopelessly tangled.

Joe's hand closed over hers. At least this way he could stop her from worrying the old hat to death. "Let out the line, then reel it in slow."

As his voice reverberated in her ear, her skin shivered and her stomach turned over. In fact, it growled like a sea lion.

"On second thought, why don't you help me with lunch instead?" Joe asked, grinning.

"Hope you weren't relying on us to catch it," she said with a laugh, following him into the galley. She ducked her head as she entered, and waited for her eyes to get used to the shadows.

"What kind of bait were you using?" Joe asked, letting the door swing shut behind them.

"More to the point, what kind are *they* using. I've been baited all morning. Questions about how much I like it here and whether I want to stay."

"Don't you?"

I do, was her first thought. She squelched it as being too suggestive. "You know I like it," she said.

"I can't know unless you tell me."

Her heart pounded as he stood very still, very close, waiting for her response. She wished it were easier than this, easier than searching for words to say when you weren't even sure what you felt. Anything had to be easier than putting your heart on the line.

She found some paper plates to busy herself with. "What are we making? For lunch, I mean?"

The two of them worked steadily, moving back and forth from the refrigerator to the stainless steel sink and countertop. There was a bedroom tucked under the prow. Behind a short curtain she glimpsed a triangular mattress resting on a raised platform. The front deck formed a low ceiling over it, a skylight in the center.

Joe caught her gaze. "Like it?" He smiled and her heart melted.

"A person would have to crawl into it."

"And be careful about sitting up too fast."

"Mmm." Obviously he'd spent some time there. "Very cozy."

"*Intimate* is a better word."

She watched the moving light the porthole cast on the blue bedspread. She pictured a starlit night and the quiet rock of water, Joe beside her, above her, the sound of water and rhythmic breathing. She had to force herself to make plain conversation. "Isn't it a bit cramped?"

"I've managed in it."

"Doing what?" The question was out before she could call it back. Her cheeks colored. "And to think I believed that sob story about the ladies not liking you around here."

He grinned, joining her at the counter. When he brushed a leg against hers, she poked him in the ribs with an elbow.

"Does Jack like mustard on his sandwiches?" he asked innocently.

He'd better, Susannah realized. She'd just slathered on a quarter inch of it. "I don't know. I'm sure Machiko does. Know, that is."

"Attentive wife?"

"I don't know if it's her or the culture she was raised in. Might just be marriage. People get to know each other pretty well."

"In spite of different backgrounds?"

Susannah nodded carefully. "I think that's true, Joe."

"Sometimes people don't know each other as well as they think."

"They have to give it a chance."

"Or give up altogether."

She knew that flat tone. "What made you so cautious? Was it a woman?"

"A woman and her corporation."

"You loved her?"

"I'm not sure anymore. We worked together. I liked her style, her confidence, her ambition. She knew the corridors of power and how to travel them. However, the answer to her dreams wasn't me, it was a V.P. in London."

"She left you for someone else?"

He laughed without smiling. "She took a promotion to vice president/finance in Great Britain. Then she very graciously, very tactfully, shunted me aside. I'll give her credit, it was as neat and clean as a razor cut." Only when she'd gone did the bleeding start.

He was smoother after that. Suave. More cold-blooded about his choices. Cautious was right. Drained of their passion, money and power quickly lost their appeal. He was on firmer ground here, where he belonged, working at building something that would last. So why was he falling for a woman who could tear him up just as surely as Marie had?

"Do you think my career is going to interfere with us? Is that it?"

"Would you let it?"

She weighed her words as carefully as she placed a garnish on the plates, folding napkins beside them. "It does mean a lot to me." There was a kind of permanence only success could buy. She could stop traveling, leaving people behind.

Joe touched her back. Reaching up under the bottom of the sweater, he touched skin. She tensed. "Afraid we'll be caught?"

"Sounds like something a teenager would say." No matter how she joked, the sensations he was starting in her nerve endings were thoroughly adult.

"I've wanted you all along, your pale fire, your warmth."

He touched her cheek with the backs of his fingers. It wasn't the sun that put heat there, nor the darkness of the galley making her pupils grow wide. He doubted it was the dryness of the day that made her moisten her lips with the tip of her tongue. His mouth had to find out.

His kiss made her melt. His tongue filled her mouth, fueled her passion. Pressed in tight, his arms captured her like a hunter seizing his prey. His body promised to fill her, a feast for the asking.

A deck chair scraped and creaked outside. Susannah's hands flattened against his back, where they had found their way to his shoulders.

"You don't want anyone to know," he said quietly, his jaw tight. "Are you ashamed of me?"

"No!"

He believed her, though it would have been easier not to. Shame would have been as good an excuse as any to stop needing her, wanting her.

She stepped out of his arms, picking up the lunch tray.

"Somebody's going to get burned if she's not careful," he said with a growl, placing the fisherman's cap back on her head.

Hat tilted at a rakish angle, Susannah stepped blinking onto the sunlit deck. "Lunch, everybody," she sang out, wondering if her voice sounded as rusty to them as it did to her. Did her lips look as kissed as they felt? No one seemed to notice.

With a wink to Susannah, Jack flipped up the corners of the brown bread to check out the coldcuts. Machiko scolded him and continued her reminisence about the trees and islands of Japan.

Accepting compliments on her delicate painting of the island opposite them, she finished her sandwich and made an announcement. "Now I want to do the boat."

"This boat? How?"

"From the island, of course."

"Sounds good to me," Jack put in. "We can take that rubber life raft and row over there."

"You just ate," Susannah said, sounding more sensible than strictly logical.

"The weather's clear, the water's calm," Jack said in his heartiest sailor voice. "We'll take our life jackets. It's only a slip of rock, so there can't be any bears, can there, Joe?"

"The only bears out here are the Sleeping Bears."

"Sand dunes," Jack explained to a startled Machiko.

"Maybe you should let sleeping bears lie," Susannah ground out in exasperation. Their completely transparent attempt to get Joe and her alone wasn't going to work.

Even when Machiko came right out and said, "Let's let the young people have fun by themselves," Susannah didn't believe it would work.

When they cast off, waving from the soft swells halfway to the island, she still didn't believe they'd pulled it off. Joe, all silent contemplation, wasn't saying a word.

She put her hands on her hips, watching him diligently checking the lines. Taking a long deep breath, she scowled at the sky, the island, the bobbing raft, watching Jack jump into the water to drag it up on the tiny crescent of beach.

Well! She wasn't about to be maneuvered like this. She hauled out one of the reclining chairs and proceeded to sunbathe. The sound of the waves splashing softly against the hull should have been all she needed to relax and enjoy the afternoon.

So what if they were alone?

Joe was keeping busy.

So would she.

First she pulled off her sweater. A boat in the blazing sun got warm fast. She plucked a bottle of tanning lotion out of her own small tote bag. She'd work on her tan. No more pale face. If she had to, she'd get brown in one afternoon.

Then she unzipped her shorts.

The noise of the metal zipper was like the roar of the engines. Joe's back was to her. If he paused while restocking the drink cooler, it was only because he was choosing the right mix of sodas to beer. It had nothing to do with Susannah stripping.

She had a bathing suit on underneath, a shiny pink maillot. If the legs were cut a bit high in the thigh, and the V front a little low, that was simply the style nowadays. Or so he told himself.

She spread a towel and got comfortable on the chaise. Fifteen minutes passed in silence. "There's a lot of puttering to do on a boat, isn't there?" Susannah finally said.

"Mmm."

"Mmmmm," she repeated after him.

He was working up a sweat with all his polishing and neatening. Lying there, feeling her own skin prickling with heat, she watched the perspiration form a line down the back of his shirt. Spikes of black hair clung to his forehead. "Are Jack and Machiko still on the island?"

Joe looked up. "Yep."

"Thank you."

"I thought you'd be glad to be rid of them for a while."

He stood over her, blocking the sun. The sud-

den shadow made her skin shimmer. She raised
one arm to shade her eyes and looked up at him.
Her stomach felt suddenly hollow, her heartbeat
reverberating inside as if her chest were an echo
chamber.

"Hot?"

She wasn't sure if he was asking or comment-
ing. Before she could speak, he pulled his shirt off
over his head in one movement, exposing bronzed
skin covered with a sheen of sweat.

She lifted herself on one elbow, aware of what
that did to her breasts, how they swelled in the
deep V.

"What's that?" she asked suddenly. One of the
fishing poles was bent and rattling in its holder.

Joe's face was stony as he turned and walked
over to the drag in the line. "Somebody's got a
catch."

Susannah got up and went to stand beside him.
She watched as he hauled in a trout, its scales
striped and multicolored. It slapped weakly against
the surface. Before she could say "poor thing,"
Joe had expertly extracted the hook and tossed it
back. With a twitch and a splash the fish dove,
then darted away in the clear water.

They sighed in unison, then smiled.

Susannah gave Joe a hug. "You've got a heart of
gold."

He shrugged it off but let her touch him. She'd
get in a lot of trouble if she thought he'd ever be
easy or sentimental. "I'll catch it again someday,
when it's bigger."

She imitated Machiko's scolding frown and
wagged a finger at him.

Joe got the point. She wasn't hugging him anymore. She was playing "just friends." He tugged
and tested the anchor chain, then stalked around

the deck, cleaning, pretending. The occasional breeze on his bare skin made his nipples tight. Avoiding the redhead reclining in the middle of his boat made another part of him tighter yet.

If they were playing "look but-don't-touch," he'd respect her distance. That didn't stop the gnawing, restless feeling inside him.

Watching her wriggle to get comfortable on the chaise, he could have sworn she was just as restless.

Six

Joe knew he ought to take it easy on her. She was more delicate emotionally than she showed. It was a kind of bravery, her reaching out to him so openly, responding in his arms every time he touched her.

If she needed time, Joe would give it to her. That meant employing the patience he'd cultivated the last three years. On the other hand, honesty meant showing her how he felt, dropping this charade that she was a woman he didn't want. From the hotness of his blood to the ache in his gut, he knew that was a lie.

He sat beside her, holding a paper plate of potato chips and sandwiches. "Want to finish some of this?"

"Sure."

Susannah balanced on an elbow, her breasts filling out the top of her bathing suit again. She considered lying back down, but with him hovering over her, why tempt fate? Unobtrusively, she tugged at a strap.

Joe licked salt from the corner of his mouth.

There was no shyness in his gaze, only undisguised appraisal and approval.

Her potato chips went down like shards of glass.

He was barely a foot away. His skin was hairless and smooth, stretched over taut muscles. His nipples were deep brown, like milk chocolate.

"Beer?" he offered.

One was too many this early in the day. She felt woozy and dizzy and distinctly tingling without it. Her equilibrium was in enough trouble. "Whatever you're having."

"A lite."

He reached over to the cooler. She caught a whiff of after-shave mixed with sweat, as she had on the hill when they'd been climbing—and kissing.

Would he smell like that in bed, flecked with sweat, his body raised over hers?

Twisting the cap off a bottle, he handed it to her. "I should have brought chilled glasses."

Her smile was as wry as his was sly. "This'll be fine, I'm sure." She drank it from the bottle, her lips conforming to the opening. The atmosphere was suddenly charged with electricity.

No sense turning into a sex maniac just because they were alone, she thought as the wind blew gently over her bare skin and his gaze traversed her legs.

"You don't drink much," she noted, taking another gulp. Harmless conversation had to be safer. When he looked up, she had the eerie feeling he could see straight through to the thoughts in her head—as if the images she wrestled with were as clear and erotic to him.

No wonder Ottawa etiquette prohibited staring directly into someone's eyes.

"I used to drink, but now I only do socially." He stretched himself out on the deck beside her. Balancing on his elbow, he matched her length for length, his legs crossed at the ankles.

"You stopped?" she croaked.

He picked at the bottle label with his thumbnail for a moment. "Having a drunk for a father was strong incentive not to make it a habit."

Her swallow this time wasn't due to the chips or the beer. "Joe, I'm sorry."

He concentrated on the bottle.

"I've heard alcoholism is a problem on reservations. I didn't know—"

"Alcoholism is a national problem, not just ours."

He never sought any kind of pity, not for his people or himself. Susannah accepted that. "I was thinking of you as a child. Living with him couldn't have been easy."

Sea gulls had found the food. They circled and cawed, splashed down and bobbed in the waves while they waited.

Joe weighed how much he could afford to tell her. If she wasn't sure about being seen with him, what would she think of the whole story? "My father hated the reservation, hated his Ottawa blood. Why he married my mother I'll never know. But he wanted a better life, and she wouldn't go, so he took me with him."

"Your mother agreed with that?"

"What mother would? But the opportunities elsewhere were undeniable. I took full advantage of them and got the success my father couldn't get for himself."

"I'm sure he was proud of you. I've heard you were quite successful."

What else had she heard? "Family is more important to us than material things. He broke that bond."

"And you never will?"

"I won't go back again. I can't."

Joe was quiet, his jaw set. He could look very fierce, Susannah thought, as he had when leading her from the craps table. He could also look very lonely. "You won't ever get divorced," she stated.

"Have to get married first. But yeah, I want to be married forever. My children will have a family and community to support them. That's why I came here. I want to make things better so no one will have to leave like my father did." He didn't keep the shadings of regret out of his voice.

"What did he think when you came back?"

The answer was harsh and quick, as if he'd asked himself the same question too many times. "He raised me to be a white man, to deny three quarters of my blood. What do you think?"

Pushing the paper plate away, she sat up and drew her knees together. She had to lower her head for a moment. "Whoa, this sun is making me dizzy."

That fast the hat was back on her head. "I told you to keep that on."

She made a face. "You're not wearing one."

"I've been under the awning most of the day. Besides, you don't want your skin to be as wrinkled as mine."

"Those are character lines. They look . . ." She was going to say sexy, exciting to the touch. She was astonished to find herself reaching for his face. She drew back.

She nervously rubbed her shins, which were smooth and covered with tanning oil. It made her think of his skin and how much she wanted to touch him. She was surprised when he picked up the conversation again.

"Money. Promotions. Résumé-building. I wanted all of it for a while. Marie included."

"You're telling me a lot today."

"There's a lot we don't know about each other. We'll have to learn if we're going to be lovers."

Susannah tried to think clearly around the catch in her throat, the throbbing acceleration of her pulse. "I'd tell you my life story again, but I think you know most of it. Lots of moving around, never settling for long."

Joe silently agreed, he knew enough of that. "What about your future? More of the same?"

A gull cried. To Susannah it was a wail of longing. If she was destined to always move on, was it fair not to let him know? "Maybe we'd be better off as friends."

"I failed that test the first time I touched you."

She barely found the breath to form a laugh. "You were trying to arrest me."

"And you were trying to seduce me."

Yes, she had been. She finished the beer. A shot of bathtub gin would have gone down smoother. "You're on the council that oversees the casino. I'm setting up the accounting procedures. That alone should be reason enough for us to stay apart."

"There's hardly a tribe member within a radius of ten miles who isn't related to the casino in some way. Would you refuse to associate with all of us?"

"Having Jack here makes me extra aware of ethics. It might be misconstrued if we were seen together."

He had a way of playing with the bottle in his hand. Tipping his head back, he drained it, the corded muscles of his neck brown and outlined in the increasingly harsh sun. His tongue caught one last drop on the rim, and his hand closed around the neck, his thumb dipping inside. It made a sound like a thunk deep inside Susannah.

Did she know her stomach rippled when she drew in a breath and held it, Joe wondered. Or was it tension, because his gaze was holding hers? "Decisions are made by consensus on the council," he argued softly. "We all have to agree. One man can't sway them."

It all sounded so reasonable. Yet Susannah knew there was a reason they should stop now. With Joe leaning closer, she just didn't remember what it was.

He touched her ankle, tugging it to the side. Then the other. With one hand he spread a towel for her. He wanted her to lie next to him on the deck. Wordlessly, she complied.

He stroked her body. Wasn't this what she'd wanted, lying beside him like this? The two of them were alone, all discussion tabled. The true communication began.

He let down a strap, drawing it over her shoulder. "Do you mind?" he asked.

She didn't say no, didn't say anything. Her breath was stopped somewhere between her heart and mouth. Maybe his hand on her breast had captured it. Revealing the pale mound with its smooth nipple, he simply looked for a moment, murmuring her name.

Her body was coiled, ready to melt or implode as he scraped a rough finger back and forth over the rosy center of her breast and white never-tanned skin.

"You're burning."

She was. She was on fire.

"Stay here." With that he stood up and left.

Susannah flopped back with a melodramatic

sigh. "Where else would I go?" she asked the bare blue sky. She tugged up a strap, dipping her chin to her chest to see the clear demarkation of pink and white where the suit stopped. He was right, she was burning. He was also a sadist to leave her.

Returning from the galley, he squinted toward the island. The raft was still beached. Jack was lying on a towel, Machiko perched on a rock, drawing pad on her knee. For someone who wanted to paint this boat, she was politely facing the wrong way.

Kneeling, Joe filled his palm with sunscreen lotion. He began with Susannah's foot. Her eyes snapped open.

"I can do that," she said, awkwardly reaching and holding up her suit at the same time.

"So can I."

He calmly proceeded up her ankles, her shins, her thighs.

"I don't want to sneak around," he said, voice rougher than it had been. "Not to do this."

"Me neither." Her voice was ridiculously high, childlike. She brought it down with an effort. "I'm not ashamed, Joe, not of you. It's what other people might think. Although I know that sounds shallow."

He finished with one thigh and moved to the other. "Being ashamed and worrying what people think sounds like the same thing." His fingers reached between her legs, the lotion cool and honey-smooth.

"It'd be like having an affair," she said, wanting to move her thighs apart. Or knot them together.

The one-piece suit covered her abdomen, so her shoulders and arms were next, then the top of one breast.

"An affair," he muttered. Not what he wanted, but what else could he give her? "Clandestine. Dangerous." He moved to the other breast.

"Very dangerous," she said softly.

He smeared two dabs across her cheeks like war paint, then smoothed them in. "Exciting?"

She nodded. The dot on her nose didn't make her laugh. She was too keen, too anxious for his next move.

Maybe it was the way she licked her lips; it made Joe realize lotion wouldn't work there. His mouth might.

His lips met hers, tested, and took. It was up to her to pull him down, to insist he lay his sweat-slick body on hers.

Her breath came in short gasps when he pulled his mouth away, seeking the fine hairs at the base of her neck.

Was it the sun that made skin sizzle against skin? She wanted to know. Her suit was peeled to her waist by his urgent hands. She wriggled to be free of it. He stilled her, having found the space between her thighs with his hand, slippery with lotion. His thumb moved material aside and explored, fast and bold and knowing.

She arched and gasped his name. She didn't know what was more shocking, his knowledge of her or the chuckle that accompanied it.

Pressing her down with his chest, his mouth took in her cry. Deep and shuddering, it made his own throat constrict. There were things he wanted to tell her, things he wouldn't know until he heard himself say them. Need, want, sharing. Could a man put all that into an affair and walk away when it was done? Was he that kind of man?

He rolled off, leaving her breasts bare to the sky. She started to protest, but he hushed her, staying close. He wouldn't hurt her, that much he knew.

His voice reverberated in her ear, soothing, enticing. He said, "lay back," and "let me," and some Ottawa words. Velvety, guttural words that were as arousing as his touch.

Susannah tried to cling to something concrete as she spiraled higher and faster. Only half his words penetrated her brain, but one had to mean "deeper" or "again."

He cupped her, caressed, a circling motion setting her on fire until her entire body was centered in the palm of his hand. His mouth devoured another cry. He could have devoured her whole, and she wouldn't have cared. She was drowning, pleading, sinking so deep her only fear was that he would let her go, or that once surrendered, she would never break free.

It was eleven that night. The sky was light, that everlasting indigo seen only in summer. Susannah lay on the bed in her condo, on the cool cotton sheets. Her body felt hot, itchy from the sunburn.

She didn't see the quill boxes on the window ledge, the birch baskets standing sentinel beside the dresser. Tossing restlessly, she saw blue sky where ceiling should have been. In the dusky room she felt the heat of the sun on her skin. The cotton sheets were scratchy beneath her. If she listened hard, could she hear the squeak of a plastic lounge chair and Joe's whispered commands? All of it was imprinted on her body, her mind.

If she wished long enough, maybe she could forget the feel of him, the intimacy she'd allowed, and the intimacy he'd refused to take for himself. If she reasoned hard enough, maybe she'd convince herself it was only lust. If she fought it, maybe she wouldn't fall in love with him.

The sound of her own voice came back to her as clear as the day had been, the sky. "What were those words you said?" she asked him afterward, breathing shallowly, feeling lightheaded.

He smiled his dangerous smile. "My Ottawa words? Burn. Fire. Fly, little bird, fly."

"Yes," she said aloud to the empty room. Lying in bed, staring at the ceiling, she was still coming down from that soaring flight.

He'd gone into the galley to get her a robe. She'd followed him. It was stuffy in there. It hadn't mattered. With a quick glance toward the island she'd pulled the curtains closed. They'd had sun and sky, now she'd wanted dark and private.

Gently wiping back her sweat-damp hair, he'd wrapped the robe around her shoulders. She'd shrugged and let it fall.

"We aren't finished," she'd said, her legs still shaky, her blood sizzling in her veins. She'd rested her forehead against his shoulder and wrapped her arms around him. There were goose bumps on his skin. Her palms spread over the flatness of his belly, the hard thrust of manhood behind the metal zipper her fingernails had clicked down.

He'd stopped her with one word. "Susannah."

Her fingertips skittering along the waistline of his shorts had made him take a sharp breath. That's when she'd dipped inside and found him, hot and smooth and ready.

But the look in his eyes had been fierce, uncompromising. "I should have known this would happen," he said, struggling for control. "I should have brought protection."

She'd thanked him for his concern with a peck of a kiss on his collarbone. Then she had to taste his salty skin. "We could do other things."

His eyes were as sharp as the sky. "You think I have that kind of willpower? I couldn't lay back and let you—" He'd stopped at the very thought. Or maybe it had been her touch that had made him grit his teeth and bury his fingers in her hair. "Not this time, Susannah."

There had been no easy way to back off. Embarrassment had flitted across her face. She'd never been one to do this casually. The easy, sophisticated way some women would have stepped back didn't work for her. Nor for Joe, she suspected. She'd picked up the robe and wrapped herself in it.

"I didn't offer this cheaply, Joe. I don't want you to think— I never have— Not without—" Without love. Was that what they had? Or had Joe stopped her to prevent it getting that far? "I mean, nobody said anything about—"

She'd stumbled, and it had been painfully obvious. She'd given something he couldn't return.

"You don't have to explain," he'd said.

But she'd had to. It had been the right time for that talk, the one she'd been practicing about how they weren't all that different. Love had to start somewhere. "I haven't had many lovers. It's hard when you're never in one place for long." She'd tried to make her smile wry, her shrug as nonchalant as she could.

"I've always wanted to make a lot of money," she'd continued. "No, not for the obvious reason. I wanted to be able to live anywhere I chose—not have someone else moving me around, like Dad with the army. So I end up with Whitman, Jablonski, and they move me every six months. Bright, huh? I envy you your home, Joe. I really do." How had she digressed so? Heavens, she hadn't wanted him to think she was throwing herself at him.

Finding nothing to clean up, to busy herself with, she'd looked in the fridge.

"When I met her, your mother said I was a migratory bird. I nest, but at many points along the journey. That was very wise. I make friends, yes, I flirt, but that doesn't mean I'm easy."

"I know."

Those had been the few words he'd said. In bed, Susannah blinked and studied the baskets against the wall. His mother. His people. His distance. Was it uncrossable? Had she gotten through to him at all? He'd said so little, then Jack and Machiko hailed them from the raft and the afternoon passed in a barely remembered blur.

Funny, she remembered every word Joe had said. Every touch.

She closed her eyes but sleep didn't come.

The casino was bustling, a typical Saturday night in June. Joe was still smarting from turning Susannah down. She'd offered. He'd been clumsy about it. He'd seen the flicker of shame on her face. As if they'd done anything to feel ashamed of, he thought disdainfully. As if she believed he thought less of her.

He'd loved the way she'd reacted so quickly, been so uninhibited at his touch. She trusted, perhaps where she shouldn't. He wanted to respect that vulnerability, the openness. With Jack and Machiko on board, there'd been no time to explain any of that, or his reasons for saying no.

Next time.

The thought stopped him in mid-stride as he

headed out onto the main floor. The next time
he'd be prepared—for the mechanics of lovemaking anyway. Emotionally, all he could promise was
to treat her right until it ended and she went
away. What then? She could lift that chin and
pretend she was fine, that past relationships were
safely in the past. But she'd been hurt before,
deeply, and if all the cultural barriers lined up
against them succeeded in keeping them apart, if
the relationship failed, he didn't want to be the
next man to hurt her.

Maybe it'd be smart to stop before they got in
too deep. They hadn't reached the love stage, but
he cared, more strongly than he was comfortable
admitting.

She'd been right in a lot of what she said. They
were both migratory birds, outsiders trying to fit
in. She fit with him just fine. He wanted her more
than ever, but there were greater differences he
had to keep in mind.

Joe scanned the casino, his hand curling into a
fist in his jacket pocket. For instance, what would
the reaction be if he came in there with her on his
arm?

He scowled and looked over the crowd, fighting
the urge to straighten his bow tie. He'd retied it
four times already. One more innocuous thing to
keep his mind occupied.

But the issue wouldn't go away. He studied the
main floor of Manitou Lodge, table to table.

Rick would be no problem. Nicky, no. Nor William, although William would no doubt keep his
opinion to himself. Everyone who met Susannah
liked her. She wasn't overly friendly or false. She
worked hard to make sure she knew every name.
She had a kind word for the folks who arrived at
six P.M. as she left each day. The Briefcase Lady,

they called her. There was no Ottawa word for that.

Joe wondered if they'd heard the story of how it had been stolen, or if that was just a nickname. Mona wouldn't have told.

And what would Mona think?

Or Jack, if word got around? Joe had to know if he'd be hurting Susannah by making her his.

The sound of loud male laughter penetrated his musings, grated on his nerves. A man in a double-breasted Italian suit stood at the craps table. A drink in one hand, he was telling the woman next to him how to throw sevens.

Joe took a left turn to the bar and got a quick refill. He crushed some ice between his teeth. It made a spot on his tongue numb. He wished another part of him were as numb.

The man was busy racking up losses. The croupier swept away another stack of blue chips. The man tossed a chip after the stack in disgust.

The worst kind of gambler, Joe thought, betting bigger as he lost. And getting nasty about it. It was time to walk over. If he got him away from the table for even ten minutes, he'd save him a few hundred dollars. Not that he wanted to prevent the tribe from benefitting, they didn't get high rollers like this every day. Big losers and big winners had their downside: Other gamblers stopped playing and started watching.

"Hello."

The man looked up, scanned the tux, the Indian features, and came back to rest on the blue eyes. A crafty kind of recognition dawned. "You must be Joe Bond."

Joe was caught off guard for just a moment. He turned on his professional smile. "I am. I was wondering if I could buy you a drink, compliments of the house."

"Sure."

The man didn't move. Joe indicated the way to the bar.

"If you insist." The man stuck out his hand for a quick, careless handshake. "Sanderson." Then he added, "Keith."

"Nice to meet you, Mr. Sanderson. You seem determined to enrich the tribe. Maybe I should say thanks."

Joe gave Nicky the order, and they were handed their drinks.

"Maybe I should thank you," Sanderson repeated, lifting his glass in a toast. He didn't. After a few moments he said, "I believe you and I have something in common."

The smirk was concealed by such practice, Joe almost convinced himself it wasn't there. He braced himself for an insult, some tasteless remark on half breeds. "How do you mean?"

But Keith was off on another tack. "How was the fishing today?"

Joe tried to remember him from the marina. No one came to mind. "You have a sailboat?"

"No, but you're the owner of *The Sporting Chance*. Or so I gathered from Jack."

"You know Jack Hainford." That explained the big-city suit.

"I work with him. Would've joined you on your charter today if I'd been invited. As I recall, Susie didn't want me coming up this weekend. She called specifically to keep me away. Why do you think that was, Bond?"

For one minute Joe felt as if he'd been hooked deep in the throat, played out slow, then jerked taut. Keith. He was Susannah's former lover, the very public affair.

"Makes a man curious when a woman tries so hard to put him off. So I came up to see what trouble she's been getting herself into." It was said with a laugh, but an unmistakable sizing up, man to man, was going on.

"Jack and Machiko Hainford ordered the charter," Joe said.

"Of course. Jack thinks the world of our Susie. How does she strike you?"

"I think that's my business," Joe said flatly. If Sanderson didn't get that smirk off his face, he'd be the one struck.

"In my line I've found that 'it's my business' is practically an admission in its own right. So tell me, how was the fishing? Or do you want to hear some of my fish stories?"

"In my line," Joe repeated carefully, "I've found most fish stories are lies. Let's leave it at that."

Joe's voice was cold and low. The Ottawa traditions about treating one's guests tied his hands, preventing him from beating Sanderson senseless right there. Of course, he could blame it on his one quarter white blood. But Keith got the hint.

He backed off. Leaning on the bar, he scanned the crowd. "You know what this place needs?" He gestured toward the croupiers and dealers. "More blondes. I know, I know. The idea is to employ Indians, but nothing spruces a place up like a blonde. Or a redhead."

He grinned. He looked like a Northern pike, all teeth.

Joe put his drink down on the bar and walked away. He didn't want to find out what he was capable of if he stayed. Marching down the corridor to the back office like a man on the way to his execution, he clenched his fists hard enough to hurt.

It took all his control, but the only thing he punched out were numbers on the office phone. He'd spent the evening thinking about Susannah. He wanted to get her down here, now, to get Sanderson off the premises. Before somebody snapped.

Seven

"I think you'd better get down here." Not so much as a "hi" or "did I wake you?"

Joe's voice was deeper on the telephone. Susannah closed her silk robe around her and realized she'd never heard him on the phone before. Or sounding so angry. He acted as if calling her were something he'd been forced into.

She glanced out the glass doors of the bedroom to the marina beyond. His boat was dark.

"I'm at the casino," he said, startling her by following her train of thought. "I want you here."

I want you. A command. Not the way she'd imagined it said. "What's the matter?"

"A friend of yours is about to get his head knocked off."

"Not Jack." She couldn't believe it.

"Keith."

The silence was a long hollowness on the line. The way Susannah felt. "What is he doing here?"

"How would I know," he said with a dismissive growl.

More silence.

Bristling, Susannah tightened her sash again. So what if the bed was rumpled behind her, her skin still heat-soaked with memories of Joe's urgent whispers? Keith was a mistake, a lingering embarrassment, but that didn't mean she had to pay for him the rest of her life. "What Keith does in his free time is none of my business."

"What he does down here is mine. I can't guarantee there won't be trouble." No more than he could promise he wouldn't pulverize the son of a b— "I suggest you get down here, Susannah."

He hung up.

The steady drone of the dial tone was like a heart monitor gone flat. Susannah stared at the phone before slamming it down in a huff. Keith! And Joe was just as maddening.

She dressed deliberately. She'd see to whatever was happening at the casino, then she'd have to see Joe Bond about this tug-of-war he was making of her heart.

Slipping on the blousiest linen she owned— anything light over skin that tingled at the slightest touch—she frowned in the mirror. Wanting anything too much was dangerous. People moved on, things changed. She of all people should know better by now. "Susannah, when will you learn?"

Be careful where Joe Bond is concerned, a voice had warned.

But careful had never been her style.

If she gave too much, she faced the consequences. All too often she moved on. But she'd never wall her emotions away, never.

She abruptly tossed the linen into a heap and pulled out her red dress, a blazing suit of armor. Keith was firmly in the past. If he didn't know that, he soon would. So would Joe. She refused to have this hanging over her head anymore.

She'd go to the casino in style, chin high, back straight. The wind-tossed hair would be easy to manage. After that afternoon it was as tangled as her emotions.

Joe set the phone down, still hearing the remote chilliness in Susannah's voice. He hadn't followed through this afternoon, hadn't been able to take that final step, to make love to her, give her some idea of how she made him feel. Touching her had been a hundred times more intense than he'd expected. It threw him, made him wish for things he couldn't have. That's why he'd kept his distance. The emotions she created in him were a wave that could knock him down and drag them both under.

Joe prowled the four corners of the back office. He knew damn well that clawing sensation in the pit of his stomach was left over from this afternoon. It was sexual, plain and simple, a biological need he should have looked after at the time. Instead, he had let it linger, making him restless, ready to lash out. He was in no mood whatsoever for civilized behavior.

In other words, Keith Sanderson picked the worst possible moment to knock on the door and invite himself in.

"Sign says private," Joe snarled.

Keith had his hands in his pockets, the suit jacket falling neatly, the lapels smooth against his trim chest. He slicked back his hair with a palm.

"It's still in place," Joe said bluntly. "Like the sign."

Keith pondered a moment, smiling a villianous smile. "There are quite a few things one would like to keep private. Somehow they never stay that way."

Joe's eyes narrowed. "What the hell does that mean?" But he knew damn well what Keith was referring to. It wasn't the thought of him touching Susannah that made something shrivel in Joe's gut, it was the idea of her responding.

She was an adult, dammit. So was he. They were both allowed their pasts. For a second Joe tried to comfort himself with the idea that she wouldn't have gotten anything out of it. That fantasy faded fast. Not Susannah. She would have cared, given, and given more.

And this slime would have taken full advantage.

"We have nothing to talk about." It was the polite equivalent of *shut up*.

"No?" He acted surprised. He ran his fingers along the edge of the desk until they squeaked. A less confident man would have had the sense to leave. "Is she why you're tense?"

He was tense because he wanted so badly to break the guy's neck. "Get out."

"You're some kind of bigwig on the council, aren't you? I could put in a good word for you."

Joe snapped quietly, like a snake rearing before it bites. "Fetch what's left of your money and get out of here before I break your—"

Susannah gasped, recovered quickly, and drew her mouth into a tight line as she stepped onto the threshold. "Would one of you mind telling me what's going on here?"

Keith turned toward her but Joe's gaze never left his prey.

"You don't know?" Keith questioned, strumming his fingers across her bare shoulder. "It seems clear enough to everyone else."

She arched her shoulder away from him and slid past him through the narrow doorway to stand in front of the desk. "Keith, what are you doing here? Does Jack know?" Score one for her.

"You made such a point of keeping me away, I had to come. Isn't that part of a woman's charm?"

Joe was the wrong person to ask. Susannah took back the initiative. This was her problem. "Not this woman. I called because I don't want you interfering in my life. Not at the office, not here."

"But, babe, you can't very well stop mutual friends from comparing notes." He tilted his head Joe's way.

Susannah blanched for a second. She wouldn't put it past Keith, but she trusted Joe. Is that why he looked ready to kill? What had Keith been telling him?

Her voice shook, as did the finger she pointed at him, but she wasn't backing down. "You are not going to have me screaming, crying, begging you to keep things quiet. I am not going to let you push those buttons. The past is over, I can't change it. As for Joe and me, that's . . . our business. I don't care what tales you drag back to the office. Let people make their own judgments. I just hope they consider the source of the information."

"End of lecture?"

"Like the man said, get out."

Keith shrugged and sauntered out. "*Ciao*, kemosabe."

Susannah wanted her legs to carry her to the sofa, but they wouldn't move. She wanted to look at Joe, to ask what Keith had told him. She didn't dare. "I'm sorry he came here."

The words spurred her to some motion. She sat heavily on the clammy vinyl couch below the window air conditioner. Cold air fell on her bare skin. The office she'd called home for a month was suddenly foreign, cluttered, and dusty. The paneling was old and cheap. It looked like she felt.

"What can he do?" Joe asked. "If he does take this back to the office?"

She looked at him a long time. They were both wrung out. "He can spread it around. Like fertilizer. Make it sound dirty and underhanded."

Joe rounded the desk and pulled her up by the shoulders. "I told you, anyone on the reservation knows I can't be bought. Not me and not the council system."

"Keith could make *Romeo and Juliet* sound tawdry. I can't apologize for my past, but I'm sorry, sorry he hurt *us*."

She had no idea how easily she could curl her manicured nails around his heart and squeeze. Until this moment, neither had he. He gave her a gentle shake, surprised he still had it in him to be gentle. "What we have isn't dirty. All he's got are rumors. What's the worst that could happen?"

She shrugged, trying to keep the frisson of fear out of her voice. "I could be taken off the account and called home."

Joe paced the office, more frustrated than ever. Home. The place he feared she'd choose over him. But she couldn't leave. Not yet. They weren't finished.

Susannah looked at the sorry state of her nails. After a day's fishing they were a mess. Like her life, they were chipped and missing quite a bit of polish. "My career with Whitman, Jablonski would be over."

Joe wasn't listening. He had no more patience, wouldn't wait any longer for a consensus of two. This afternoon she'd made him an offer. He was going to take her up on it.

He picked up the phone and dialed the bar. "Nicky? Have a bottle of champagne ready. And get Bill G. in, I'm taking off for the night."

He took Susannah's hand. For a moment she believed it was the only thing holding her up. "I'm sorry for all the trouble, Joe. Perhaps we should stay away from each other."

"Until this dies down?"

There was electricity in his grip, an elemental force that connected them every time. What they had would never die down, not when just a touch singed her like this.

"We could call it quits." She tried to let go.

His grip was unrelenting. Something in his eyes dared her, made promises she didn't want to hear. If he wouldn't let go of her hand, at least she could break eye contact.

"I'll be leaving in a few months. If not sooner. It might be better for both of us—"

"It would be bull." That got her to look at him. "You're coming with me."

He tugged her halfway down the hall before he stopped himself. He had to be patient, not the way he'd learned to deal with the tribe, but for her sake. They were going to do this right if it was the last thing they did, or the last night they spent together.

"Watch your step."

Susannah carried the spike heels in her free hand as they walked down the dock planking. Barefoot, her step was as quiet as his. He set down the champagne and hoisted her up the ladder. *The Sporting Chance*. His last chance, theirs.

She lifted her skirt to step over the rail. The slit helped. So did his coming up the ladder behind her.

"Go," he said.

He didn't touch her once they were on board.

He threw off the ropes and pushed away from the dock. A green and a red light flickered on either side of the marina entrance. Climbing to the bridge, Joe flicked switches, running lights, choke, radio. The engine broke the darkness with a rumble and roar. He cut it back to a deep growl.

The floor shook, Susannah noticed. So did her limbs. He'd rushed them there, assuming she'd come along. He'd assumed right.

With the wind tugging her hair, pins were pointless. They hit the black water with tiny splashes. The spangled dress shimmered like moonlight only deeper, darker. She looked like a bloodred mermaid on her last night before the spell was broken.

The boat hugged the shore, the scent of pines drifting their way. Engines grumbling, they prowled the shoreline until the casino lights blinked out behind the trees and darkness enveloped them. After fifteen minutes Susannah glimpsed a small bay opening before them.

Joe cut the engines and they drifted silently. He brushed past her in the dark. "Look out." That's when they came to a stop, the bottom of the boat hushing up on a sandbar. Joe dropped the anchor overboard for insurance. The chain clanked, and the rope hissed through Joe's hands like the time they might have together. It stopped quickly in shallow water.

"Joe?"

She came up behind him. He could feel her there. She'd been inside him all day, those fluttering lids, the clutching need, the invitation in her voice this afternoon. . . .

Taking what she offered now meant more than physical release for him. He'd have to be a complete heel to pretend he could walk away from this woman. He'd have to deny everything she made him feel. The question remained whether he could openly proclaim her his woman, let everyone see he hadn't left the white world entirely behind. But he couldn't let her go without this one night.

"You're like a flame in that dress," he said, turning. "Like fire."

He found her hand and held it inside the jacket. Although he had to fumble for it, he undid a stud and pressed her fingers inside the shirtfront. "Feel the heat you make, Fire Woman?"

"I do."

"You have any ideas how to put it out?"

"Everything I think of would only make it worse. I hope."

His chuckle made her quiver. Considering the heat coursing through his veins, he doubted she'd ever quench what he was feeling. He led her through the door into the blackness of the galley. Even stars couldn't outline them against the indigo sky.

"How does this come off?" he asked gruffly.

"Simple."

Waves tapped the hull of the boat and clucked far away on the sand, the pines whispered, a zipper slowly unzipped. The dress was a puddle at her feet. She stepped out of it and into his arms. No lace, no silk, just her—warm, pliant, and naked.

"You knew this would happen," he said.

"I got dressed in a hurry. At your command, as I recall."

He felt her chuckle as his mouth searched the slope of her shoulder, his fingers tracing a path down her spine. "I needed you. Does that make me weak? Disloyal to my past?"

She shook her head, unable to find the words when her mouth was busy rediscovering the hard line of his jaw, her fingers unlocking the mystery of shirt studs. The bow tie she'd already figured out and removed. "I can't imagine you weak."

"Wait till we're finished. I'll be like a newborn kitten."

She pictured what it would take to make him that way. She swallowed.

"I don't know what to promise you."

"Then don't say anything." She could be as honest and blunt as he. She reached around him to undo his cummerbund. He found the closure at the front of his slacks. Two pairs of hands found the zipper.

"I can't imagine you tame as a kitten." She smiled in the dark. "More like a mountain lion. Something that sees at night."

"And hunts by scent." He buried his face in her hair, then found her mouth. The kiss was long, deep, and fulfilling.

The galley was small. They were no more than a few steps from the bedroom tucked under the prow. The rings that held the short curtains tinkled as he pulled them back. Susannah recalled the triangular mattress on its shelf. She had to step up, then lie down. Joe ducked her head with his palm. "Be careful." His hand glided down her waist, her hip, memorizing the way she reclined.

There was the sound of his shoes hitting the floor. Musty smells of boat and trapped heat. Her eyes adjusted to starlight glittering through the porthole. She reached up and opened it, letting in the breeze and the night sounds, listening to him rummaging through his clothes.

He joined her, letting her touch him everywhere, smoothing, murmuring her compliments in return for Ottawa words or simple sounds of pleasure. He touched her thighs, she tensed.

"Are you sore? Did I hurt you?"

She shook her head, knowing he'd feel it in the dark as her hair brushed his arm.

He skimmed the back of his hand over her breasts—heated skin, cool mound, tight peak. He placed his palm over her eyes and switched on the dome light.

She blinked.

He scowled. "You've got quite a burn."

The line crossed the tip of her breasts. "I look like Neapolitan ice cream," she muttered with a grimace and a laugh.

"Pale faces should be more careful. And pale breasts."

"Must have been exposed to the sun longer than I thought."

He placed a tender kiss on each breast. "These have never been exposed."

Not in the way they were to him, she thought. She shook her head, fighting off the fear that he might withdraw again.

"If I lay over you, it will hurt," he said.

"We'll be careful."

He looked into her eyes. *Careful* was not in his vocabulary right now. The patience, even the humor, were costing him. "You could be on top. You could straddle me," he said huskily.

The simple statement made her insides turn to honey. She wanted to reach out but hesitated at taking the lead. "How?"

He scanned the space as if seeing it for the first time. "No room, is there?"

There was hardly room for him to raise up on an elbow. His head brushed the ceiling, his bicep bulged, a vein throbbed, and she had to touch it. He quivered, and she took heart. "Any other suggestions?"

"First, something for that burn."

He left her, but the light followed. She watched the taut muscles of his back, his behind. He didn't have the tan line most men had, those white cheeks. It had always seemed so childlike to Susannah, like a suntan lotion ad. But not Joe. He was no child when he turned, standing before her.

"You like to look," he said, pulling down the corners of a smile.

"It's rude among the Ottawa, isn't it?"

He couldn't hide his pleasure. "Not in this situation."

She loved that smile. With a sigh she returned it. Love. Easily said and easily acknowledged when it came to something as simple as a smile. She traced his full lower lip, the lines that bit deep around his eyes. There was gentleness there, earthiness, humor, and blatant desire.

He opened the tube of moisturizer, squirting a line of white between her breasts. She gasped at the cold. His smile became tight. "Hold on, *squandeh*."

The next line was a slow circle drawn on her abdomen, then two lines for each thigh. The creme tingled, cooling the burn with a burn of its own.

It was incredible, the erotic, stimulating contrast of dry skin and lotion, smooth hands and the rasp of calluses. Her body was limp, but her insides were rolling like stormy water. She'd scream if he kept this up.

Joe watched her, jaw tight. He'd put sunblock on her thighs today; they weren't as badly burned. Between them her nest of red hair was as creamy as the lotion coating his hand.

But he had a job to finish, protecting and caring for his woman. The feeling shook him. Swelled him. Tonight she was his, and he wanted her with everything he had.

She moaned. His hand couldn't stay away, stroking, soothing. It was he who was being tortured. Why? Why was he punishing himself? For the sake of love play? Love? That might explain why all the vows in the world hadn't kept him away from her. But thinking would come later.

Her legs parted as he sought her. She touched his face, his shoulder. She found his chest, the black hair surrounding his manhood. His entire body shuddered.

He reached to the window ledge, hands shaking. With one hand slippery from the lotion, he used his teeth to tear open the cellophane packet.

"I could have done that." She smiled lazily, deliciously.

He put it on. "You could've made me stark raving mad too."

She chuckled. Another shock to his system. She was stretching him to the limit. He gingerly picked up the tube of lotion again, aware that control was a tenuous thing—unlike the sure grip of her hands exploring him.

He had planned on rubbing in a thin line down her hip.

She planned on repeating his every motion with one of her own.

"Susannah," he said on a groan.

She smiled. Heartlessly. Ruthlessly. Incredibly pleased. "But I want to."

"And I want to last another thirty seconds."

This time when he groaned, she laughed, her body shaking. He squeezed the tube flat, a white puddle of tingling coolness on her abdomen.

She reached past him to switch off the light, and the stars seemed to come streaming in.

The sound of his breathing was harsher in the dark. He lowered himself on her. Their bodies spread the lotion, sliding, gliding, catching on the dry spaces. It was like the sound of a wet kiss, a boat parting water with its prow.

It was the feel of her thighs on either side of him that broke his control, the touch of his tip to her molten core.

If it was too fast, she didn't say. Her few scattered words were lost in kisses and cries and tiny bites she spaced along the shaft of his neck.

The smell of cocoa butter mixed with the astringent smell of lotion and musty air, cool water and a summer night. They could have been in a cave, on a forest floor. The first man and woman, primitive, uninhibited.

Their bodies found the words, catching the rasp of a tongue, a grunt. Savage peaks were reached, only to be followed by breathtaking plummets, unreachable crests, all at once and all over again, until the final demanding thrust, the joined shout. An ever-receding wave washed them on the abrasive, fine-grained sands of a night shore, clutched close in each other's arms.

Eight

He'd wanted to take her the way no man had, to places only the two of them had been. Looking in her eyes, he knew he had.

The doubts didn't come till later, when he was in the galley opening the champagne. As much as it choked him to say the words, he had to ask if she'd been as shaken by their lovemaking as he.

Susannah came up beside him at the sink. "You're being quiet."

"I'm curious about why a woman like you would be attracted to me."

"Whoa, there. I'd have to know exactly what's involved in being a 'woman like me.' "

Joe grinned, but it lacked the teasing quality Susannah expected. "You're beautiful, exciting, you live in the fast lane."

"You're painting with a mighty broad brush, partner. Thinking our worlds are too far apart?"

He didn't answer as he worked the cork loose.

Susannah shook her head in amazement, answering his question as directly as she dared. "It's you, Joe. That's why I'm attracted. You're honest, direct, you know precisely who you are. You don't have to use people, or climb ladders, or impress anyone. . . ."

"Tell them that." The twinge of bitterness surprised him. So did facing up to a truth about himself. "There's a lot of reserved judgment going on about whether or not I'll stay. I'm considered too modern, too pushy." The women who'd rebuffed him because of his foreign ways had been telling him something he'd chosen not to hear.

Susannah told him something else. He was fine as he was, her world and his could mix. When she returned his long looks, she made his heart sputter. Dammit. What was he going to do with her? The cork popped, fog curling out of the opening.

He could try not to hurt her. He'd always promised himself that. He could argue with her about things she couldn't understand. Love her until he was too exhausted to turn thoughts like this over in his mind anymore. "Champagne?"

Susannah took the glass he offered, feeling the easy intimacy fading. She'd come out here to stand beside him, naked and suffused with satisfaction. Now she picked his pleated shirt off the floor and put it on. She didn't bother with the buttons. It stayed closed when she let it, swayed open when she moved. She retrieved the glass from the counter, aware of his steady gaze as it darkened. "What are we going to do next?" she asked.

"Besides make love until we're wiped out for the next week?"

She meant the future, the one they both had to face. But futures to her had always meant moving on. If she wanted this to work, they had to reach a deeper kind of intimacy. She had to understand

Joe Bond and what was important to him. "You think your people don't accept you."

He ran a hand down the sleeve of the shirt she wore, more than a little distracted by the way she filled it out, the way her thighs peeked from the tails, the occasional glimpse of a mound of soft red hair. "I was away too long. They don't believe I'll stick around."

"But you will."

He nodded. "I made a promise to myself, a vow, if you believe in those things."

She did. And she knew without a doubt that Joe did.

"I wanted to help, to improve things."

"And how do I interfere with that?"

Joe winced at her choice of words. Honesty was the right way, but it had a way of hurting, and that was the last thing he wanted to do. "I've wondered what the tribe would think if I took up with you."

"Took up?" She smiled at the phrase.

"If I were seen with you. Going in your condo at night, or coming out of it in the morning."

She sucked in a breath. He'd obviously given it a lot of thought. She was pleased, even flattered. She was also disturbed. "You could have been as compromised as me that morning we were on the boat," she realized suddenly. "You certainly handled it well."

He nodded. "There was nothing to be ashamed of."

"And there is now?"

He didn't answer. The champagne had to be corked or it would go flat.

"So you care a lot about what other people think." It wasn't as tactful as Susannah would have liked, but it got to the point.

"No! If they don't believe me, I can't be effective. I can't accomplish anything unless they trust me. *That's* what I care about." He took a deep breath and lowered his voice. "I can make a difference here, even if it's one brick at a time. No one should feel compelled to leave. Families shouldn't be torn apart, scattered." He was getting close to the bone now.

"It has a lot to do with my father and me. I don't want that happening to me or my wife and children."

Susannah wondered wistfully whether he included her in that thought. "So I'm the kind of woman you can't be seen with." It wasn't a fair crack, but she wasn't feeling terribly fair.

The pain in her eyes was fleeting. Joe reached for her anyway. His fingertips brushed fire-red hair off her damp cheek. A curl wound around his finger, dipping into the glass she held so close to her chest. He picked the strand out, drawing it between his lips, sucking it.

"Is that your conclusion, Joe? You don't want to be seen with me because it threatens your standing in the tribe?"

"No." All these words and he still hadn't explained it right. She threatened him because he wanted her. He wanted her so badly that there were times he didn't give a damn about the tribe. Sometimes it was merely need, a deep, gut-aching need laced with a loneliness that quit only when they were together. Or when she looked at him. The way she was now.

"I'm going to have to face up to, or face down, a number of people," he heard himself saying. "They'll have to accept the fact that I want to be with you."

"Don't let me ruin your reputation, sir." The Southern accent took him by surprise.

"It'll probably confirm what they already think of me."

She shook her head. "You've worked hard to get this far. I don't want to endanger that."

"I'll work harder. It'll take longer. They'll have to be tolerant."

"Will they?"

"We're known for our tolerance," he said with a grim smile. Patience and more patience, that's what he'd need. And Susannah looking up at him with that bed-tossed, hand-mangled head of hair, framing a face out of a fantasy. She made him feel as light-headed as a dozen glasses of champagne. She made him feel love. No matter how naive, optimistic, or empty-headed it might sound, he was sure they could work it out if they had that.

At the look on his face, Susannah's stomach flipped, like champagne bubbles bursting all at once, or frantic butterflies let loose. His palm cupped her cheek, and he said three words softly in Ottawa.

Funny, Susannah thought, the words *I love you* sound the same in any language. Caution gripped her heart, cowardice too. She wanted to look away before he caught the fear in her eyes, the hope.

"You keep saying things I can't understand. Those words you said this afternoon, for instance." Not these words, anything but these. She understood them all too well. Maybe she wasn't as ready to face the future as she'd thought.

"I'm not sure what I said." Joe pondered his admission. He'd never been in so far over his head that he hadn't known what he was saying. He remembered this afternoon, this evening, trying not to grow hard at the erotic memories. He sensed her retreating; he'd have to play it cautiously.

"*Qua*. That means woman." He called her his woman.

"Is that all?"

"Does any man need more?"

She smiled. He was joking. She was safe.

"*Squandeh*."

She remembered. "Red."

"Another one for you, *ninimoshe*."

That last one she'd heard before, this morning when he'd slapped that hat on her head. "Wear this, *ninimoshe*." They'd been friends then, without all the risks being lovers entailed.

Susannah nuzzled in close, giving him a hug, aware it could ignite much more than friendliness between them. The shirt opened, letting skin touch skin.

"How does that lotion feel?" he asked, his voice dry.

Head back, hair falling loose and full down her back, she matched the devilish look in his eye. "Think we rubbed it in sufficiently?"

"That should have done it."

"You might have missed a spot."

Teasing he could take, but the wanton way she swayed with the boat's rhythm had him wanting to open her mouth with his, part her legs.

"That's a great way to change the subject." Extending his unwilling arms, he held her away. "You stopped asking about us."

She dropped the hug, letting out a laugh even she didn't like the sound of. "I never said I could stay, Joe. Not beyond the year it would take to set things up. One month is gone already."

"You don't want to stay?"

She touched his bare arm. "I just can't promise, that's all. I'm a migratory bird, remember? A classic love 'em and leave 'em type."

Hardly, Joe thought, watching her flit nervously around the room, looking at the countertop, the tabletop, even the damned tackle box, before she looked at him again.

He was being put off. Gently, tactfully. He hated every minute of it. He was used to getting his way. Perhaps fortunately in this case, he'd had some practice with perseverance these last three years. He might find it in him to let her back off if she needed to. "Haven't you ever wanted a permanent relationship?"

"I thought so once. It was ironic, though. When I wanted permanence, he didn't."

"Who was he?"

Her pause answered the question for both of them. Keith. Considering the scene tonight at the casino, Susannah felt she owed Joe the explanation. "For a long time I told myself that I'd been using him, too, to teach me how to fit into his kind of social circles. It wasn't true, but it helped."

Joe nodded for her to continue, wondering how much harder he could clench his teeth. He didn't want Sanderson intruding.

"The bottom line was that he was in Chicago. Permanently. I thought he would be my center, someone I'd return to after my travels. He'd be home."

Joe scowled into his drink. It was the most unlikely description of Keith Sanderson he could have imagined. "I must not have seen what you saw in him," he drawled.

Susannah smiled, but it was at the countertop, the table, the tackle box. "I can really pick 'em, can't I?"

You're fine, Susannah, he wanted to say, pulling her into his arms. Instead, he played it light, the way she did, anything to make it easier on her. "You picked me."

"Brilliant, huh? Here I am never settling down, and you're as rooted as a person can be."

"A single person," he corrected her.

They left that one hanging.

"So you're tired of this place already," he said.

"You know I love it."

I love it. Not I love you. He waited, hoping the silence would make her say more.

"It's just that I've learned not to count on staying anywhere for very long. That's life." She bit down the longing that sprang out of nowhere, the longing for a family, a real home. She suddenly wanted promises, she wanted to be asked to make them. But could she keep them, considering the pattern of her life? Always moving on? "You chose your place in the world. I guess I've chosen mine."

Before he could stop her, she was through the door and out on deck. She gestured to the sky when he followed her out. "See the moon?"

A sliver of white moon rose over the water. She wanted Joe to look at it, not her. He understood, but that didn't stop him from putting his arms around her. She tensed.

"Shh, *ninimoshe*. Stay here."

Stay. Susannah told the vise gripping her heart that one word wasn't a long-term invitation. He wanted her in his arms, that was all. For now. And for now she'd stay right where she was.

He trailed a line of kisses under a shirt collar that smelled of his cologne. Susannah tilted her head, baring her neck to his lingering mouth. "Never made love to my own shirt before," he whispered.

"I could take it off."

Although he stood with his bare back to the

cool night breeze, his skin grew hot. He peeled off her shirt and it fell with a whisper into a pile on the deck. He touched his chest to hers, pressing her breasts between them. Only a word from her could stop his hands from marauding over her flesh. "Is your skin still tender?"

"My back is."

"We didn't put lotion there."

"No." The word came out breathlessly, a contradictory invitation.

"Then come into the water with me." He took her hand. Holding the rope ladder away from the side, Joe let it clatter into the water. He swung his leg over the rail. "Stay inside my arms."

Her foot met the water. "It's cold!"

"It'll feel good on your back. Stay on the sandbar. Don't let it get any deeper than your waist."

Susannah expected sand at the next step. Instead, she plunged off the ladder into four feet of water and came up sputtering. "Oh, my Lord! Is this your idea of a cold shower? This is frigid!"

"It's wonderful," he said with a laugh. "You'll get used to it."

"That's what Attila the Hun said to the conquered hordes of Asia."

"We can swim, but not far."

She hated to admit it, but the cold did feel good on her back. Now, if only her teeth would stop chattering. "Do this often?" she asked petulantly as she gingerly lowered herself to her chin.

"Not often enough." His hands were on her waist, her legs bumping his in the black water. That quickly the blood rushed through her veins, hot meeting cold with nothing but watery resistance between them.

"When did you take your clothes off?"

"I never swim in a suit," he said.

"Never?"

He licked droplets off her cheeks, her neck, her breasts. Wet and cool, the water brought her nipples to tight peaks. So did he.

He touched the backs of her thighs, silently showing how he wanted her. With a catch in his throat, he felt her legs go around him and drew a ragged breath. He slipped inside her, surrounded by warmth.

It was slow this time. Exquisite and maddening. All he could do was stand there and hold on.

"I'm going to have to pull out," he said tightly.

She heard him. She just didn't listen. He was so hard, so full inside her. She felt the way his body quaked when she tightened around him. She wanted him there, inside, until the last possible moment. And when it came, she wanted him to stay.

"Don't go," she breathed in his ear. "Please." Her legs twined around him, her arms. Her hands held back his hair, her tongue tantalizing his ear.

"I can't protect you."

"It's not important, not now."

"Susannah."

"Now, Joe, please."

His thrust made water splash and clap between them, ripples unreeling on the surface of the water. They were in the center of the whirlpool, breath catching and rushing out, building like a flash flood, harsh and guttural and hot and wet. When it subsided, he held her in his arms, the sand shifting under his feet as he lowered her, only their foreheads and hands touching.

"Is this sweat?" she asked, untwining their hands to run her fingers over his forehead. She could still hear his breath in the dark, labored and heavy. She lifted a handful of water and poured it down his face. When she lifted another handful, he dipped his head and drank from her hand. The rasp of his tongue on the center of her palm made her go still inside.

"I'll take you home."

Why she'd ever agreed to go to Mona's for dinner, Susannah couldn't fathom. "I'd like to take you out to dinner sometime this week," Joe asked her as he docked the boat that night.

It was such a conventional request, it surprised her. "Of course."

He walked her down the dock to her door. He was being distant again. She suspected there were things he wasn't saying. She wouldn't push. So much had already been said. "Anywhere special in mind?"

"Mona's."

His mother's? She gulped, sinkingly aware she'd already said yes.

"Now what?" Susannah muttered the following Saturday as she slapped another dress onto the bed. "Too businesslike. Too dressy. Too flimsy. Why did I bring *that*?"

Pacing, looking at her watch, deciding the watch didn't go with the dress, taking it off, putting it back on so she could glance at it in case the evening dragged, Susannah was a wreck, and it was barely seven o'clock.

She ran her hand through her hair, mussed it, then decided it would look better in a bun. "A bun! You're meeting the man's mother, not applying for a job!"

A job interview would have been easier. How did one reel off one's résumé to somebody's mother?

The doorbell rang. Susannah cursed, once again fighting with the clasp on her watch. "Good evening," she said as she opened the door.

Joe stopped in mid-stride halfway across the threshold. "Good evening," he responded just as formally.

Susannah didn't catch the glint of humor in his eye. She was too busy looking him over. Jeans. "I'm overdressed," she said.

"I can think of a way to deal with that," he murmured.

"You didn't say it was casual."

"We're only going to my mother's." He was growing as tight and tense as she was.

"I'll have to change."

"I'll wait."

"Fine."

Closing the bedroom door behind her, Susannah released a pent-up breath. Lord, what were they doing? Acting as awkward as blind dates on prom night. She'd met Mona, for heaven's sake. Mona was welcoming and friendly; she was also curious and didn't mind saying things out loud. Unlike one close-mouthed man Susannah happened to know.

She slipped on a casual off-white jersey and switched earrings. The tan sandals would have to do. Her hands were shaking so badly, she was sure she'd snag her nylons undoing the straps if she tried to change now. She took a deep breath and opened the door to the living room.

Joe turned. That was all that was necessary.

He looked her up and down, nodding slowly. He smiled. For one heart-skipping moment Susannah wasn't sure they'd make it out of the condo.

He said nothing. He didn't have to. He could undo her with a look or a word.

"Ready to go, *ninimoshe*?"

Sweetheart.

Her heart melted, then the rest of her, remembering his arms around her, her heartbeat mingled with his. Sweat, water, breath and mouths and tongues.

She wet her lips with the tip of her tongue. "Ready as I'll ever be."

If he didn't stop looking at her like that, they'd be late.

He offered her his arm. She found her purse. They were on their way.

Nine

Mona greeted them at the door, the smell of stew floating out to them. Susannah realized she'd been so nervous, she hadn't eaten since breakfast. "It smells marvelous."

"Venison stew. I thought I'd make something you don't get in Chicago."

"Thank you, but my dad's a hunter. I cried at *Bambi*, but it never stopped me from loving venison."

That quickly Mona and Susannah were engaged in a long discussion of spices and stews and the best way to prevent the meat from tasting gamy.

Joe stood back and watched them take turns sampling the bubbling stew. The women couldn't have been more different—one short, round, and dark, with her thick braid falling down her back. The other lithe and redheaded, with skin like pale fire, her cheeks highlighted a sun-burnished pink. Yet for all their differences, they were cut from the same cloth. They were both open, generous, friendly around strangers.

Susannah was right about making herself at

home anywhere she went. She set the table, comi-
cally scowling at Joe to lend a hand. His mother
gave short commands in Ottawa, telling him the
same thing. He didn't know who to watch more
closely. Would Susannah be accepted? Mona had
set him up with a number of arranged dates in
the last three years. Never had he brought one
home of his own accord. What Mona thought would
give him a strong indication of how the rest of the
tribe would feel.

"You didn't even taste that stew," Mona chided
Joe later.

She and Susannah were clearing away the dinner dishes.

"A million miles away sometimes."

"You've noticed that too," Susannah agreed,
laughing. She touched his hand.

How could his mother not see the love there, he
wondered.

"Oh, Mona, I can help wash those."

"They can sit. Let's go outside while it's nice
and cool."

They retired to lawn chairs, Mona carrying strips
of birch to weave into a basket. The moon was
thin but strong enough to cast shadows in the
clearing. The faint sounds of television sets murmured from the other trailers. They settled in, the
motion of Mona's hands rhythmic and confident,
the steady scrape of papery wood ancient and
soothing.

"Joe told me he spent his summers here."

"Every year," he said, "learning the legends."

"Is there a legend about the moon?"

"Legends about most everything and how they
came into being," Mona said, threading a green
piece of dyed wood into her design.

Susannah laughed softly, a sound that rippled

over Joe's skin. He reached for her hand. "All we need is a campfire," he joked. Her answering squeeze did little to ease his tension.

"Long time ago," Mona began, "Mother Earth and her children lived happily. Brother Sun and Grandfather Moon took their turns day and night. But the moon got jealous. He wanted to be bright and warm too. The great spirit told him to be content. You can't have everything you want."

Joe shifted in his chair. He'd heard this story all his life. The words should have been familiar and comforting, not filled with new meanings.

"Grandfather Moon snuck up on Brother Sun to steal some of his light. When he stood between the sun and Mother Earth, he blocked the sun's light."

"The first eclipse?" Susannah guessed.

"Right. But sun's heat forced the moon away. To this day, he keeps trying."

"I like that. Do all the legends explain natural events in such human terms?"

"Many do. They tell you about nature as well as people."

After a few silent moments Joe got up. He paced to the edge of the trailer, standing on the edge of the dark.

"Could we hear another one?" Susannah asked.

"There are lots of them," Mona said. "Hard to choose which one is just right."

"I'll be back," Joe said softly. With that, he prowled toward the perimeter of the clearing, like a foraging bear. His tension was palpable, even at a distance.

All Susannah picked up from the next story was something about when the crows had their feathers painted black.

"Well?" Mona asked directly.

"I'm sorry, Mona. I missed half of that."

"I know. I'm listening to myself talk tonight. Where do you think that son of mine has gone?"

"Into the forest?"

"Sulking."

Susannah sensed how high the stakes were, the price Joe would pay if Mona refused to accept them. "Won't he get lost?"

"He's found his way home from farther away than that."

Joe had found his way back from miles and years away. "What was he like as a little boy?"

Mona turned her face for a moment. Her words were short. "When he was here, he was a good boy. Sometimes I don't think he dealt with the split very well."

"The divorce, you mean?"

"The split inside himself. Between the world his father wanted him to have and this world."

"What was his father like? If I'm prying, Mona, stop me, but I want to know, and there's so much Joe keeps inside."

"His father and I were very much in love. But he didn't love this place. He wanted Joe to have more. Sometimes I think he gave him less."

Susannah thought about that. She gathered her courage. "I love Joe."

"I can see that."

"I think he loves me."

"I think so too."

"He's worried what everyone will think."

"Is that it?"

Mona kept working, threading her basket. Her fingers were deft and fast, but she was slow to impart confidences.

"Maybe Joe should talk to you about all this," Susannah suggested.

"Then he should come talk."

They listened to the crickets and the distant traffic. Joe appeared at the end of the trailer, his steps so soft, Susannah was startled to realize he was there watching her. A thrill akin to fear or excitement made her shiver. Perhaps it was the darkness he seemed to carry with him. If he needed to resolve this with Mona, she'd give them privacy. "I think I'll go inside a minute." The screen door slapped shut behind her.

Joe's low voice carried to where Mona sat. "The moon stealing the sun's light. What was that supposed to mean?"

"You know the story. It's one of our legends. It explains things."

"It's about going after what you can't have. About opposites not being meant to be together. It's about getting burned."

"Then it's full of lessons. What do you want, Joe?"

"Susannah." The answer was so simple. It scared him how much he needed her, like the moon needed the night air to suspend it. It was what he needed, not necessarily what he was entitled to.

Mona continued weaving one strand after another, dark then light.

Joe came toward her. The sound of water filling the sink came through the kitchen windows. So did the sound of Susannah humming. She might be able to relax, but Joe was wound tighter than a reeled-in line. "I promised myself when I came back that I'd stay. I promised you."

Mona shrugged as if that weren't the important part. "Do you mean to stay?"

"Yes."

"Then what's the problem?"

"I also promised I'd marry within the tribe."

Mona waited. The shadows grew short as the moon rose.

"How can I promise who I'm going to love?" Joe blurted out.

"No one holds you to that. Those are promises you can make only to yourself."

"Doesn't that count?"

"It means if you break the promise, you're the only one you have to settle with." She rose to go inside, settling her supplies in the bottom of the newly formed basket.

"I want your opinion."

"She means very much to you. You love her. Can you live with that, Joe?"

"Can you?"

"I don't have to. But I'll say this, I don't want you torn in two like your father was."

He bit back a reply and looked out into the dark. "So you're saying I shouldn't marry."

"Don't be trapped, that's all."

He cursed. "She's not out to trap me."

"I'm not insulting her, she's fine. I'm saying you must choose what you want most, Joe."

"Dad chose to leave. And ended up hating me because I couldn't. I had to come back. This is part of me."

"He was part of you too. He felt half breed, so he wanted you whole. He thought he could do that by removing the Ottawa in you. But you came back, and I'd tell you legends. It was part my fault. I wanted you to be part of me too. You made a very brave choice."

"I turned my back on him. Isn't that why he killed himself?"

The words hung in the air. Mona stood on the metal stairs until the chorus of crickets resumed.

Her hand curled around the railing. "He was divided. What he did is not your fault."

"I don't want to do that to my children."

"What about her? Maybe someday she'd want to leave."

It was a possibility he'd feared and would have to face. Until their relationship had more time to grow, he couldn't expect any promises, any long-term plans. What about children? He couldn't answer that until he'd asked her. "What will the tribe think?"

Mona shrugged eloquently. "I can't speak for them. They have wondered about you, whether you'll go back."

"I can't, you know that." He'd made the choice. Like his father's death, there was no turning back.

"So stay. Same with that woman. If she loves you, maybe she, too, will stay. Love can be simple if you don't put too many conditions on it. But that's enough wisdom for tonight. Why don't you walk her home before she takes to cleaning my kitchen cupboards."

Joe didn't laugh, although the sounds of Susannah putting away pots and pans could be heard clearly. He watched the mosquitoes buzzing by the yellow porch light. Respect made him listen. Frustration made him want to storm away.

"You want my approval, Joe," Mona said, interrupting the silence. "I can't give it."

The words cut through the air like an arrow—swift, sharp, painful. Joe turned before she finished.

"Ever since your father took you, you've been outside the boundaries. You're half her world, half ours. You have to decide for yourself."

•　•　•

Full of questions, Susannah didn't ask how it had gone with Mona. Barely a word passed between them as he led her through the woods. It was the way he claimed her that night in bed that told Susannah everything.

He was desperate and greedy as he kissed her good night. His body quivered like a bow string at her touch. They were inside her condo as quickly as her shaking hand could get the key to work. His arms went around her, rough and demanding. Clothing was discarded, the bedspread tossed aside as they tumbled onto the sheets.

For the first time they were actually in a bed, Susannah thought. But the fear that gripped him threatened them both. It snuck into the room, huddled in the corner and waited.

She loved him and she wanted him to know. Pinned beneath him, plundered by his intensity, she knew she could answer his need, and so there was no fear. Except for his sake. What price was he willing to pay for their love? Would be ostracized? Shunned? Would their children be? She had to ask. But she had to give first.

Sounds of desire emanated from her throat, soothing, enflaming. Her mouth made its way down his chest, feeling the muscles jump and flex beneath her wanton tongue. She tasted the tangy sweat that beaded on his skin. Hard and taut, she tasted his power, felt the blood rushing through his body like a primitive drumbeat. He shuddered and moaned. Clutching fistfuls of her hair, he drew her head back.

"Woman, you've got to stop this." His voice was husky, it sounded angry from the constriction of his throat.

Susannah knew better. Heedless of the darkness in his eyes, a wild power had seized her.

Invigorated and daring, she sprawled across him, part heathen, part wanton, the smile on her face pure woman. He wasn't the only one able to seduce, unhinge. Tonight it was she who would brand him as hers.

When the shuddering sensations receded, his heartbeat slowed and he could speak again. "You make me crazy."

"Good." Susannah stretched languorously on the rumpled sheets.

He felt drained, and envious. How could she be so at ease when his gut felt like braided barbed wire? "You think you've got everything figured out ten moves ahead, don't you, Red? Like a fox."

"I thought that was chess."

"The fox invented chess, didn't you know that?" He laid back. Lifting his head to look at her was too much effort.

"Is this another legend?"

"No, it's the truth."

"Ah." Susannah ran her hand softly over his chest. His nipples were smooth, the chocolate aureoles still fascinating her. She wanted to lick them. She licked her lips instead, savoring his taste. "I love—" No, she would say it honestly, what she really loved was not what they'd done, it was him. "I love you."

He stroked her back, protectively touching her hair. "Don't say any more."

They lay awake for a long time, thinking instead of speaking.

Joe remembered he'd said the same words to her, but in his own language.

If she left, what would he do, Joe wondered. What would he be but an empty, discarded husk. Could he follow her, return to her world? Were his own promises that easily overturned? What if they married? What if her promises proved as empty as his?

He'd always thought of himself as a man of integrity—until she arched and called his name, plunging him into a place where he was out of control, where she was all that mattered. He was so willing to lose everything for her.

Even a child? If she left with his child, what would he do? Stay? Follow? Fight? He'd be fighting his own past. This time on Mona's side of the fence.

He knew he was looking at the black side, but the very idea made his blood run cold. You couldn't keep someone if she didn't want to stay of her own free will.

If he abided by his vow and stayed with the tribe, at least there'd be something left for him when she was gone. There would be a man walking in Joe Bond's shoes, running his charter service—a man who would never be as whole again without her.

His life had been one of choices, black or white, yes or no, here or there. These questions were harder to answer. Would she stay if he asked her? How long did love last?

Toward dawn he pulled her to him. Their love-making was torturous and tender, as if this were all he could rightfully give her.

Susannah woke alone. The curtains were drawn back, the sun just clearing the horizon. She glimpsed movement on the *The Sporting Chance*. Joe was working. He'd left before anyone could see him. Suddenly he straightened and looked directly at her. Her heart caught in her throat. Just because his blue eyes sometimes pierced her like a knife didn't mean he could see her behind the glass. Her pulse pounded anyway. Joe went back to work.

Last night she'd told him she loved him. She'd meant every word. He'd told her too, in the way he made love, the earthy intensity, the shocking intimacy. He never held back, except when it came to talking about the future.

Susannah shook off a frisson of nerves. In the shower, thoughts rippled over her body like water, like daydreams. A man she loved, a home, roots. A family. Was that asking too much? People managed it all the time.

She dried off, threading her hair into a French braid, remembering the way Mona wove strands into her basket. It required concentration. Holding the pins kept her hands steady, although the night had taken its toll on her shaking legs.

As she glanced out at the boat, the smell of the coffee Joe had started for her seeped into the bedroom. The idea that he'd been thinking of her gave her a warm feeling of sharing—as long as their sharing was done in private.

"Susannah Moran, you are not going to get clingy." Out loud it sounded a little more resolved. The man had his life. He had commitments. Could she ask him to risk everything for her love? Especially when all she risked was having her dreams come true?

She sighed and poured a cup of coffee. Lord, he made it strong. If she'd been paying attention, the sheer blackness would have tipped her off. Milk did nothing for the taste. Neither did Joe's walking down the dock at just that moment. An attack of nerves made everything taste like rust.

"Give it time," she muttered, wiping down the

counter. Patience wasn't only an Ottawa virtue, after all. Maybe the tribe would get used to her.

Maybe the summer would end before they found out.

Maybe she'd better keep living her own life and not throw everything into a dream that had never come true before.

Sliding the glass doors open, Joe stood for a moment, watching her get plates from the cupboard. Her cropped white top clung to her breasts in the morning humidity. She reached for glasses. He watched her midriff bared by the movement, her tan shorts hiked higher on her thighs. Neutral, simple colors on a complex, vibrant woman. He hardened at the sight of her.

"I like that braid."

"Thanks." She smiled.

Her smile was wide and radiant as always. The night had put extra color in her cheeks. He liked the way she walked when she was barefoot, the way her hips moved. "And good morning to you too," she said with a laugh.

Her skin was dewy, her hair fragrant and damp.

"You should put lotion on after a shower. It will help with that burn."

"Thanks for the advice," she said, although his voice was gruff, his manner off-putting. There was no way he was going to intimidate her this morning. She'd seen too much of him last night. "Care to rub it in?"

"I've got a charter at nine."

"I don't have to be at the casino till eight."

"I'll help with breakfast then." He stepped around the island.

She'd meant to tease, not push. "Okay. What're we having?"

"Whatever you've got."

She'd already given him that. She poured some orange juice while he rummaged in the fridge. "Eggs over easy on toast sounds good."

"I'll make 'em. You get ready for work."

"Want some juice?"

"I'll take some coffee. Black."

"So I noticed."

Her chuckle made his abdomen tighten. He kept his eyes on the frying pan while she puttered in the bedroom, tucking in sheets that were wrinkled and loose, picking up discarded clothes.

"I'm going to check in and see if there are any messages on the machine," she called.

"All right."

She used the phone in the bedroom to dial the casino office. There were three messages. One to call the Chicago office—the reason the machine had been installed—and two more to see if she'd gotten the first one.

She put the phone down, the words incised on her mind. They'd been so clear, she was surprised Joe hadn't heard them in the next room.

Jack Hainford's voice: "Come down to the office this Friday. Organizational meeting you need to attend. And, Susie, I want to go over a couple things with you beforehand. Privately."

Privately? Something in her shriveled. Something was up. Was Keith behind it? Did she even need to ask? He'd suspected her and Joe before there'd been anything to suspect. At least she'd credit him with a keen instinct for people, she thought disgustedly. And for working fast.

If Jack did confront her, there was no way she could deny being involved with Joe. Only that it would have no effect on her work.

It sounded hollow even to her. Would she be reassigned? Let go? The prospect had its up side.

She'd be free to move there on her own. *If* she thought she had a future with Joe. But there was no way she could spring a future on him this soon.

On the other hand, being reassigned elsewhere would stifle any chances their relationship had of growing. Her cheeks burned at the thought of facing talk in the office again. This was something she refused to see dirtied. She loved Joe, deeply and honestly. However, the time needed to nurture that love was slipping away.

"Here's your eggs."

"Thanks." Susannah wet her lips with orange juice and hoped that would make the meal go down.

"Any messages?"

"Just the home office."

She caught the small tightening at the corners of his mouth. She changed the subject. "Would you like to do anything this week?"

A million things, he thought. From lying with her to swimming, to watching her sip orange juice across the breakfast table from him every morning. All he had to do was get her to stay.

"I'll be running down to Chicago next weekend," she said spreading butter on her toast.

Until that moment Joe had no idea you could pierce a man to the heart with a bread knife. He'd been a fool to think she'd stay. She was leaving already.

"I'll probably leave first thing Friday."

He wasn't giving up. They had one week. He could take her around the bay, to the lighthouse, introduce her to all the places and people who meant something to him. Make her fall in love with more than just him. Not until he tried everything would he step back and let her go.

He loved her. More than was prudent and certainly more than was wise. She'd become part of him. There were a lot of people who weren't going to be comfortable with that. Hell, he wasn't comfortable with it. He was in knots the half of the time he wasn't head over heels. He was way past halfway measures.

Mona hadn't given her blessing. He was an adult, he could deal with that. He wouldn't deal with love on the sly. Susannah was the woman he chose. Before the week was out and she returned to Chicago, the whole tribe was going to know it. He'd let the chips fall where they may.

Ten

Every night Joe made sure Susannah was busy—
with him. They toured area wineries, the restau-
rants on Old Mission, took in a symphony at
Interlochen, a romantic walk along the bay as her
sandals swayed in her hand. Every night they
made love. Except for two days when he had fishing charters at dawn, he stayed until breakfast,
then walked down the dock to his boat.

"Aren't you worried someone will see you?"

"You're the woman I love," he said simply, watching a flush of pleasure invade her cheeks.

Direct and honest and to the point. All the things
she loved about him, Susannah thought. She
sensed he was also uncertain, feeling his way. He
was risking a lot for her. She wouldn't know
until Friday's meeting with Jack what she risked
in return.

Thursday at five Joe walked into her office at
the casino.

"And where are we off to tonight, kind sir?"

He glanced at the piles of papers and 13-column
pads on her desk. The devilish twinkle in his eye

made the hair on her skin stand up and take notice. "Think you could wear that little black dress?"

"Gladly." She slunk around the desk and played with the collar of his knit shirt. "*If* you tell me where I'll be wearing it."

The humor in his eyes was replaced by tension, the kind created whenever she touched him, or smiled, or stood so close their bodies almost touched. She was still learning the thrilling power she exerted over him.

"It's where we're going after dinner," he replied, his voice strained.

"I must have done something special to deserve all this. Was last night that special?" she asked.

He moaned, unable to take her in his arms. They'd both picked the casino as off-limits, due to her work and his volunteer job. "You know damn well every night has been special," he said.

"Sorry. I was teasing."

She didn't look sorry. She looked about as triumphant and sure of herself as any beautiful, sexual, incredible woman had the right to.

"Hell," he snorted, kicking the door closed. He dragged her into his arms and kissed her until she was rumpled and weak. Letting her go abruptly, he turned. "Seven o'clock," he said, and was gone.

Susannah took a deep breath. She didn't know whether to laugh or panic. Not yet, she decided. They had a lot of barriers to get through before she could safely laugh. And the panic about what he might be planning could wait until after dinner. That's when he'd sprung all his other surprises this week.

Each evening had ended with a visit to a house or trailer on the reservation. She'd met his aunts, various cousins, and friends. Joe was showing her both sides of his world—the community as well as the tourist attractions. Everything went well, she'd felt welcome everywhere. So why should she fret about that night?

"I've met his mother, what more can he spring on me?"

She found out later that night when they pulled into the casino parking lot.

"Here?" she squeaked, automatically touching her hair.

Joe looked at her long and hard. "You look beautiful."

He had a way of saying that as if she were the first woman the words ever described.

"But I thought we were staying away from the casino."

"I thought it was time we made it official." Maybe it was too bold a gamble, but Joe wanted her tied to him somehow. She'd proclaimed herself a rolling stone. He had to show her what community and family were like, what this place had to offer, before she went back to Chicago and started making comparisons. He had to show them both that this relationship could work out in the open.

"I should have known when you put on the tux," she said as he opened her car door. She stopped him between two parked vans. "A kiss for good luck?"

His eyes were hard to fathom in the gathering darkness. The fact that the hand gripping hers was equally tense didn't help her confidence.

He pecked her on the cheek. "Give me half a chance, and I'd rub off all your lipstick. Come on, it can't be any worse than walking into the place planning to cheat."

"I wasn't cheating, I was only switching dice."

"Interesting distinction."

"I wasn't trying to get away with any money. I *wanted* to get caught."

"To see how you'd be treated."

"Yes."

"And were you treated well?" He turned and looked at her.

They were on the front deck, outlined in light, the noise merely a background to their racing hearts.

"I've never been treated better," Susannah said softly.

Joe touched the black silk of her dress, amazed all over again what a woman could do for a simple piece of cloth, and what those black nylons did for his anatomy.

Tourists bustled through the door. "We've got some people to meet."

Even on a Thursday the place buzzed. Joe ushered them to the bar. "Nicky? I'd like to buy a drink for the lady."

"Miss Moran. Good evening."

The words were appropriately polite, the gaze averted. Either Nicky managed a quick appraisal anyway, or Joe was fast becoming the jealous type.

"What'll it be?"

"My usual," Joe said.

"On duty tonight?" Nicky asked as if that made everything okay.

Joe leaned across the bar, his face inches from Nicky's. "I happen to like watered-down scotch. Is that a problem?"

Nicky's eyes grew wide. His gaze flicked to Susannah and back again. "No. Here. Sure. The lady?" He directed the question to the bar top.

"I'd like a—"

"—diet red pop," Joe said on her behalf.

"Coming right up."

While Nicky was poking around under the counter for soda pop, Susannah surreptitiously stroked Joe's arm. "Having fun yet?"

He scowled. He'd wanted her to make a good impression on his coworkers, little realizing it was he who was blowing it. But dammit, this was important to him. Most of the casino employees knew her. This time they were meeting her as his woman.

"William," Joe called.

William Missaukee came over. "Evening, Joe. Didn't know you were on the schedule tonight."

"I brought someone for you to meet. A good friend of mine." To emphasize it, Joe put his hand on Susannah's waist.

"Hello, William. You look very dapper in that tux."

"Charmed, as always." The older man gave a courtly half bow.

Susannah laughed. This was going so much better than she'd feared. If only she could get Joe to see it.

"Will you be enjoying our games?"

"Afraid I can't. I was trying to talk Joe into letting me buy my own drink though."

"I hope he refused. Just because he has different ideas doesn't mean he lacks manners. His mother raised him right."

"And my father?"

There was an uncomfortable pause. William answered thoughtfully, "Your father took a different path."

"What does that imply about me?"

"There are a lot of paths, Joe. As long as you know which one you're on. Excuse me."

Susannah released a pent-up sigh. "What did all that mean?"

"Just about anything you want it to," Joe grumbled.

He took her arm and escorted her through the crowd to some of the less busy blackjack tables. Susannah said hello to everyone she knew. As Joe Bond's personal guest, people looked at her differently, when they looked at all.

"Word gets around fast," she murmured in Joe's ear. "Don't tell me I'm the first woman you've brought in here."

"All right. I won't tell you."

They continued making the rounds. Susannah reminded herself to lift her chin. As long as she was on display, she'd hold her head up. "What did you mean when you said things mean anything you want?"

"It'd be nice if people here were as quick to give you their opinion as they are everywhere else. Sometimes politeness and reserve get on my nerves."

They were at their last stop.

"Slow night, Hank?" Joe addressed the man operating the big wheel.

"Yeah," Hank said. He was broad everywhere, from his nose to his cheeks to his expanding chest and belly.

And none too friendly, Susannah noted. She'd seen him around the casino but had never introduced herself.

"This is Susannah Moran," Joe said.

"I know," the man replied. "You going to put down a bet?"

"Not tonight."

"Okay, then." He proceeded to ignore them, giving the wheel a turn. It clattered to a stop like a playing card stuck in bicycle spokes. "You betting again?"

"No thanks."

"Okay again, then." He spun it one more time.

Joe's grip was as tight on Susannah's wrist as it had been the night he'd captured her. Clearly, this was one person they weren't going to win over.

"Shall we go?" she asked.

"I want to talk to Hank for a minute." He looked like he'd rather hit him.

"I see you're still a *wannabe*," Hank said, eyes on the big wheel.

Susannah searched her memory for a translation of the word. From Joe's clenched jaw, she knew it wasn't good.

Hank supplied it. "Still wanna be an Indian," he said, his laugh an ugly rumble.

"That's what I get for wishing for an honest opinion," Joe growled as they returned to the bar.

Susannah was fuming, but she didn't let it show. "That was only one person."

"The only one who'd come right out and say it."

Late the next afternoon Susannah entered the offices of Whitman, Jablonski, and Parritt, wrung out from her eight-hour drive. She took the elevator fifteen floors, then chose the back stairs for the last flight. Going in the front way would mean passing Jolene. She wanted a few moments alone to gather her scattered thoughts.

All the way down she'd gone over the scene in the casino, coming up with sharp comebacks for Hank, encouragement for Joe. None of it helped. The evening had been ruined.

"But people *were* polite. I wasn't completely shut out." Just another argument Joe wasn't around to hear.

She'd been arguing it in her head all night. A thermos of coffee on the ride down couldn't wash away the lack of sleep.

"Wash away," she groaned, opening her office door. That much coffee was bound to have side effects. She set her briefcase inside the door and headed straight to the ladies' room. She needed to prepare herself for the meeting with Jack Hainford. That was another issue she'd argued all night.

She splashed water on her face, despaired of the wrinkles in her skirt, repaired her makeup, and headed back to her office, meeting no one in the halls. Arriving at lunch hour had its benefits.

For the first time in a month she entered her office. It was bare. A rush of air left her lungs as she sat in her chair. Her plants were lined up against the wall, leaves covered with a light coating of dust. Boxes were filled with her things. If she'd wondered about being fired, she had no doubts now. It was the office of a person who was leaving.

"Susannah!"

She looked up at Jack's hearty smile, determined not to cry. "Hello, Jack."

Nothing could hide the stricken look on her face. Jack patted his tie to his chest and paid studious attention to her office window. "Have a nice drive down?"

"I'll be out of here as soon as I can." She just wasn't sure yet where she'd go. She had no fight in her. Her arguments were as substantial as the dust on her plants. She rubbed the headache between her eyes.

"You must be tuckered out after the drive. Let me get you some coffee."

"No! I mean, no, thanks. I've had plenty."

"So why don't we get started?" Jack leaned on

the edge of her emptied desk. "Come on into my office, it's a little cozier than this."

Of course it was. It was the office of a man whose job was secure. A picture of his wife and family posed in front of his house on the north side sat in a prominent place on the bookshelf behind him. He was as dedicated to them as he was to this job. She'd always liked that about him.

He gave her a moment to get settled, then began.

"Pardon me?" she asked.

"I said, you've hardly said two words."

"Sorry, Jack. I feel like three of the seven dwarfs: Grumpy, Wrinkled, and Tired." She folded her hands in her lap; they were shaking. "Sorry I was so sharp about the coffee. The last thing I need is more caffeine."

Jack buzzed Jolene to hold all calls. A bad sign, Susannah was sure. She felt the defensiveness growing, and they'd barely begun. "What is this all about, Jack?"

He played with his tie and reached for an ever-present glass of water. He raised his brows by way of offering her a glass.

She shook her head. The pause only made her think of other things. If she was out of a job, where would she go? She'd scanned the local papers for jobs in the towns nearest the reservation. None of them were exactly what she had in mind—

"How is the market up there anyway?"

Startled by the way he picked up her thoughts, she took her time formulating an answer. "Why do you ask?" Because she'd be looking for a job, that's why. Jack wasn't cruel, he wanted to make sure she'd be okay. How could he know that all depended on Joe Bond?

Jack smiled. He could smile through anything, Susannah thought. "It's been discussed here in the office."

"What has?"

"The market in Northern Michigan. It's growing. You pointed that out when we drove up there."

So she had.

"Keith says you seem to be thriving up there."

She smiled thinly. "I'll bet he did."

Jack cleared his throat with a cough. "What we're looking at, Susannah, if I can get to the point here—"

"Please do."

"Is the question of whether you'd be happier out of the main office. I know Keith is still a sore point with you."

He droned on. Susannah kept her eyes on the floor. This was it. Keith, and in part her own behavior, had seen to it this would be the conclusion of her career at Whitman, Jablonski.

Jack was still talking. He could be lively and funny, but when he had a speech prepared, he could fall into a midwestern monotone all his own. Susannah would miss him.

"—which we think would be best for all concerned. We were so sure you'd like it, I had your office packed up."

Susannah was startled out of her reverie. "Like it?" How was she supposed to like this?

"You can think about it, of course."

Think about it? She rubbed her forehead again. "I'm sorry, Jack, could you go over that one more time?"

"Sure. We want you to open a branch office. You've scouted the area. I think it would be a fine place to start."

Stunned, she let him continue.

"I realize you'll be out of the main office, out of the main action. Frankly, we've been turned down before on similar transfers. People don't want to feel shunted aside. But with the casino contract, we have an in with the community. You've had a chance to scope out the place."

"Jack. I'd love it."

He looked up. "Realistically, office politics-wise, it does take you off the fast track as far as management opportunities down here. However, we won't forget you. A few years testing in your own office, and you could come back."

She stood. "On the other hand, I could stay up there for as long as it works out."

"You like the idea?"

"What I'd like, Jack, is to kiss you." She came around the desk, took his surprised face in both hands, and gave him a smooch right in the middle of his forehead. She laughed at the lipstick mark. "I'll clear out my office today."

She was flying. A branch office. A chance to set up a permanent home. She'd never dared dream . . .

She'd never even had a chance to open her briefcase. She was affixing shipping labels to the boxes in her office when Keith paused in the doorway.

"On your way out?" he asked.

"And up," she replied, whistling.

He put his hands in his pockets and slouched against the door frame. "Oh, Susannah," he crooned. She looked up. "Being carted off to the boondocks isn't my idea of up."

"I meant up north. And that's just fine with me."

"Seems to be."

"I know you don't understand it, Keith. You think what you have here is perfect. I've got something better."

He started to saunter down the hallway, then turned, smoothing back his hair. "*Ciao*, baby."

Susannah shut her door with a soft but satisfying click. Damn, that felt good. Almost ready to go. But first she had a phone call to make.

What time was it? Did he have a charter today? It was Friday. People would be taking three-day weekends. Of course he'd have a charter. Besides, what would she say if she got him on the phone? "I miss you. I love you. I'm coming back to stay."

What if he weren't ready for that? The threat of having to move every six months was no longer hanging over her head. However, his barriers were still standing. Last night proved that when it came to being accepted by the tribe, they still had a long way to go.

At least she'd be around to see how it worked out.

She glanced around the bare office. She'd tried to make this a home. She shook her head vigorously. It just hadn't worked, not without woven baskets. And there was no view of the water.

She had another meeting with Jack the next day to go over setting up the new branch, the budget, the staff. Then she had to give notice on her lease and pack up her apartment.

She dialed long distance, leaving a message on Joe's machine. "Unexpectedly delayed. Back Sunday night." She tried to keep the laughter out of her voice.

Eleven

It was Saturday night. Joe stared at the ball rolling in the opposite direction of the spinning roulette wheel. Always on the outside, like him, until it came tumbling down. Where it ended up was anyone's bet.

He glanced around the room. The other members had been friendly since he'd brought Susannah in. Except for Hank, they took it in a very matter-of-fact way—on the surface, at least.

But there was no sense in having them make up their minds, when he was in the middle of second-guessing his. He'd proclaimed her his woman in the most public of ways only to have her take off for Chicago the next day. She'd said she'd be back Saturday night. Then a message changed it to Sunday. If he'd worried that Hank's negative reaction had scared her off, he needn't have. She sounded happy, laughing, having a wonderful time. He was ready to chew bricks.

How many times had she told him she was a rolling stone? How many times had he really listened? At the beginning he'd wanted her to go, to spare herself any scars, to prevent him from making all the mistakes he'd already made. Now he'd give anything to have her back.

A few heads turned at his bitter laugh. Joe glared into his drink as the roulette ball fell into a black slot. He was the one actively seeking scars. He loved her, and he had a hopeless feeling he always would.

It had to be love. What else produced mood swings from dizzy optimism to grim determination to this limbo of waiting—all because she'd gone to Chicago for a few days.

He checked his answering machine four times a day—that he counted. All he got was Mona's invitation to another dinner. She mentioned only him. Had she heard Susannah was already gone?

Sunday night one of the blackjack girls made a joke about his being the Great Snapping Turtle. Joe chose to take offense, withdrawing like his namesake. At least it got his mind off waiting.

When she walked into the casino, he knew. Immediately. He looked up. So did half the men in the place. Joe did a slow double take, his pulse beginning that familiar thud, the slam of recognition that made his breath shallow.

She had on a black dress. Unlike the silk number, this one had lace on its shoulders and a heart-shaped neckline. Mid-length sleeves made her arms look long and willowy. Her hair was down around her shoulders, fiery, stunning. She looked like a million bucks.

Which was about nine hundred thousand more than she could ever hope to earn around there, Joe acknowledged. Just looking at her, he knew she wouldn't stay, wasn't meant to. He had to end it. Tonight. Cut short the torture of waiting for her to go the next time.

She waltzed up. He took her in his arms. Let everyone see, he thought. Let them remember with him. He had to hold her once more, kiss her for every time they'd never kiss again.

When he was through, she threw back her head and laughed, gasping for breath. Her eyes sparkled. The weekend had rejuvenated her. He wouldn't fool himself that it was the kiss.

Loosening his grip, he let her feet touch the floor. She looked incredible. She tasted even better. He wanted her so bad he hurt. He tried not to be jealous of a town, but what could he offer her here?

"Been busy?" she asked coquettishly, playing with his bow tie.

His throat constricted. "All weekend," he said, unable to keep his eyes off her.

"I thought you had a charter today."

"All day."

"Then what are you doing here? They can't work you twenty-four hours a day."

"I wanted something to do since I didn't know when you were coming back."

Susannah paused, her gaze on his tie. "Sorry about the extra day. I had—some things to attend to. I bought this dress. Like it?"

He nodded.

"Let me tell you all about it. Outside?" She waggled her eyebrows suggestively.

Setting his drink down, he almost smiled. Not ten minutes had passed, and they were leaving together. He didn't care how obvious it was.

Outside, the evening air enveloped them. "I actually got back around six," she said.

"You could've flown. I'd've picked you up at the airport."

"I wanted to drive. I had some thinking to do."

Pride. Joe figured if that was all he'd have left, he'd better hold on to it tight. "About us?"

"That too. But I want to show you, not tell you." She laughed gaily. "Come with me for a drive?"

"Anywhere. As long as it ends up at your place or mine."

She chuckled. "I never knew that line to be so effective."

He curled his fingers over the edge of the car door. "Susannah."

"Shhh." She put a dark red fingernail to his lips and danced around the other side. "The car isn't what I wanted to show you. It's going to be a surprise."

The road wound along the bay. They followed it for ten minutes until they were off the reservation and halfway to town. A new office building was going up. Construction was everywhere in the growing resort area. This one was three stories high and hugged the beach.

"They're beginning to lease space here," she said. "I noticed it the first time I drove past."

"Yeah."

Susannah got the feeling she wasn't walking on sand but on eggshells. She was happy, thrilled. For some reason she wasn't communicating to Joe. He'd been distant and hurt looking since she'd walked into the casino. If someone had made a crack about them, she wanted to know. Was she proving more of an embarrassment than he'd bargained for?

The two days away were supposed to have given everyone time to get used to the idea of her and Joe. Going to Chicago by herself meant showing them she had no intention of taking him away.

Instead, he was working very hard at taking himself away.

They parked and marked off the perimeter, side-stepping piles of excavated dirt and sand. Around the side, a few scrubby evergreens acted as preliminary landscaping. The bleached and stained wood exterior blended naturally with its location.

But the waterside was the showpiece. Glass doors and balconies for each office bespoke of light and airy interiors. Susannah pictured what moonlight would do to them. "I wish there were some way we could get inside."

"We'd get arrested."

"Party pooper." She shrugged. "Not that that hasn't happened to me before."

He scowled. "This time it wouldn't be prearranged with the management. I'd have to call William to bail us out."

"How has he been, anyway?" She was having to dig and pry for information. She didn't like it.

"Fine. We've all been fine." Joe left it at that and they explored a little more.

"It would be more private inside," she said wistfully. "We could talk."

Her soft words inflamed him. He wanted to take her in his arms and to hell with talking. "Why here?"

"I want you to picture an office here."

"When Sporting Chance Charters gets bigger, I'll lease on the reservation."

"I meant for me." Careful, a voice chided, careful. Susannah wanted to tell him, not spring it on him. Just because she was moving here didn't mean she expected an instant commitment from him. It didn't have to mean anything major. Except where her heart was concerned. "That meeting in Chicago—"

"I take it you had a good time."

"Yes. Especially after Friday night."

He stalked away so quickly, she had to follow or lose him in the dark. She caught his arm and abruptly let go. She'd promised herself she wouldn't cling. "Did something happen while I was away, Joe? Did somebody say something?"

He felt like a heel for putting a damper on her fun. She was clearly delighted to be back. Why couldn't he simply enjoy her while he had her and to hell with the future?

"Did Hank say something? Your mother? Talk to me."

"Nothing happened." It was the plain truth. Without her around nothing stirred him, nothing caught at his gut except the sound of her voice on the answering machine.

She stepped squarely in front of him and took a deep breath. "Joe, I wanted to bring you here to tell you I'm moving up here."

"You're already here."

"Permanently. Whitman, Jablonski wants to open a branch office in northwestern Michigan. I've been put in charge."

She waited for a response that didn't come. So she waved an arm at the building, chattering like a salesman. "This is the office space I was considering. It'll be perfect for our needs. In the meantime I'll be doing some hiring, pricing furnishings, finding a computer setup that can interface with Chicago."

She was staying. Joe tried to take it in.

"Whitman, Jablonski also has an intern program. And a scholarship fund."

"Is this what you want?" he asked, seeing it clearly now. He heard every word. And misunderstood. She wanted to be an executive, moving up the corporate ladder. This was the next rung.

"I've never settled down until now," she was saying. "I've wanted to."

"I'm sure you wanted this all along."

She said it out loud. "The fact that you're here made the decision much easier, Joe."

"So you got what you wanted, Susannah."

Her name sounded so formal suddenly. She wanted *squandeh* or *ninimoshe*. She wanted his teasing smile.

"This isn't *all* I ever wanted," she said firmly.

"No?"

"You know it isn't." She longed to be in his arms. Outside of them, the words were difficult, the night air chilly. "I thought this would give us more of a chance. People could get used to us. It'd make it easier for you."

Nothing could be easy because nothing could be certain. The promises Joe had made about staying weren't promises he could expect her to make. She'd stay until they moved her up again. "There are things no amount of time will change, *ninimoshe*."

She flinched when he touched her cheek. It was the gentleness, the soft regret in the way he spoke.

She clutched his palm to her face. "Is it the color of my skin? Is that it? Don't tell me you'll let that come between us."

His hand was back at his side, his eyes memorizing her as if she were far away, a vision from the past. Susannah had to reach him.

"Is it the way we were raised? You come from a broken family. I don't, but that didn't mean we weren't disrupted every year by another move."

"You said it yourself, you're a migratory bird. I'm staying."

"So am I!" Her voice shook. She folded her arms. "That's what I'm trying to tell you. I've always wanted a home, Joe. I want to make mine here."

"You didn't even know where here was until a

couple of months ago." He turned toward the water, unable to look at the pain in her eyes that he was inflicting. He'd never wanted to hurt her. "You're saying this only because you love me."

"And what, may I ask, is wrong with that?"

"My father loved my mother too. At first. Love fades. People need more in common."

She was busy wiping tears off her face. She felt as hollow as the building hulking beside them, as brittle as girders and glass.

"Is it your standing in the tribe? Is that it?"

"I've already risked that."

"And lost it?" she asked, her voice shaking.

He shook his head. He touched her cheek again. So soft. "It was worth it, Red. Every bit of it has been worth it."

"Then why?" She couldn't put the rest of it into words. Why was he leaving her?

"It's not the personal risk. It's family, children."

"I love children."

"So do I. I don't want to put one through what happened to me."

"You wouldn't have to."

"There's no way we can know, is there?"

"You haven't even asked me. I love you, Joe."

"I couldn't force you to stay."

"And you won't leave. I know that."

"But I would, dammit!" His shout echoed against the glass before he got his emotions under control. Why did the tears glittering in her eyes make her even more beautiful? "For you I'd go anywhere. I'd go back on everything I ever promised, break my word."

"Is that more important than family?"

"What do you think a marriage vow is? Breaking it destroyed my family. And my father."

Joe kicked at the sand, listening to the hush of the water.

"He couldn't deal with my returning, not after all he'd done to make me successful outside. It destroyed him. Now tell me I'm supposed to change my mind again. Tell me the white world was the right one for me all along." He looked out on the black water, the white band of moonlight laid across it. Black or white. Yes or no.

"I can't go back on this decision, Susannah, any more than he can go back on his. My children will have better lives, they'll be free to leave *and* return."

They were through talking. Susannah caught the glint of light on the satin lapels of the tux, the stark outline of his profile. "I'll walk back," he said. He turned and headed around the building.

The crunch of gravel told her when he reached the road. That's when her first sob broke free.

Susannah's mind was boggled by the hundred ways a person could fill up three weeks. She had end-of-the-month reports at the casino peppered with meetings with realtors, decorators, purveyors of office furniture, phones, and computers. Most evenings when she got home, it was too dark to see whether Joe's boat was at anchor or not.

She discounted the trouble she had sleeping as entirely due to the strong black coffee she'd taken to drinking. All day. Every day. If it made the nights longer, that only gave her more time to analyze what had gone wrong.

The finality of his words haunted her. He had to live with his commitment to the tribe. But she was willing to make commitments too, if only he'd let her. She expected him to call. He didn't. She found herself reaching for the phone more and more, the receiver in her hand, the dial tone buzzing like static, unable to press the numbers.

On Tuesday afternoon phones were installed at the new office. Susannah listened to the saleman explain the ways a person could transfer a call, hold it, conference it. But when he left, she simply stared at the phone, sleek and beige, sitting on her brand-new desk.

"There you go," the salesman had said, getting a dial tone. "Now you can call anyone, anywhere in the world."

Her anyone was barely four miles away. It could have been the moon.

Alone now, Susannah picked up the phone and listened to the hum. She punched numbers, a series of beeps, faraway ringing. She had to talk to Joe. It couldn't just end. He picked up. At the sound of his voice, her heart fluttered somewhere near the middle of her throat.

"This is Joe Bond."

"Joe," she rushed in before her nerve failed her, "we have to talk about this. I—"

"Sporting Chance Charters runs every day from May first to October first for parties up to twelve. If you would like to make a reservation, please leave your name and number at the sound of the tone, and I'll get back to you."

Susannah put down the phone before the tone could sound and sank exhausted into a chair that smelled of fresh plastic.

Of course he'd be out on his boat. It was the middle of the day. August. The bay sparkled. She wanted rain. Lots of it. "Just my luck, that would probably be great for fishing."

She stared out the floor-to-ceiling window. The decorator had alternated tall plants with baskets as Susannah requested. In the corner stood a brass telescope on a tripod. Susannah couldn't resist. She scanned the water for signs of Joe's boat, scolding herself for spying, congratulating herself for finally taking advantage of the third-story view.

No sign of him.

Not that it would do any good. They needed to talk. Hating herself for the indulgence, she punched his number again, just to hear his voice.

Joe turned on the machine. There was a click, then nothing. The silence made him think of Susannah. He imagined he heard her breathing on the other end of the line.

"Bull." He was the one who should be calling her to do some heavy breathing. He was that desperate to see her. And equally determined to stand by his decision.

Another repeat of his message, then a woman's voice sounded in the room. His heart leapt.

"You coming over for dinner, or do I have to make an appointment with my son who's so busy?" Mona.

Joe dialed her, disgusted with the way his fingers shook. He'd thought for a moment it was—

"All right, Mom. When do you want me?"

"Tonight is okay, if you're not down at the casino like every other night."

"I'll make an exception. Can't promise I'll be any kind of company."

"So be morose and snappish. I've seen that before."

Was he really getting that bad? Susannah had lightened him, balanced him.

•   •   •

"So you stopped seeing her," Mona said, picking the subject out of the air as they cleared away the dishes.

"You didn't approve of her, as I recall."

For some blasted reason the tune Susannah hummed the night they'd visited kept repeating in Joe's head as he dried dishes.

"It's not my place to approve."

"Of course it's your place."

"I want you not to be like your father. That's what I want."

"So I'll stay!" He gripped the edge of the sink, swearing under his breath. His temper was short lately.

"Stay and do what?" Mona challenged. "Be miserable? Hate your life and us too? We aren't your jailers."

"I never said you were. I chose to stay and I will. And rebuild whatever credibility I've lost. I'm sorry if you're angry."

She was tossing baskets into a pile, gathering strands of thin wood as if ordered to evacuate the premises. "I'm insulted that you think us so intolerant."

"I've worked hard to prove I'm not going back. I blew it."

"I'll say."

He looked up swiftly.

Mona's dark eyes were steady. "No one is blaming you for loving a white woman except you, Joe. You get this from your father."

"Get what?" He hated it when she stared at her baskets with that pursed mouth and that inscrutable, superior expression. She used to tease him as a boy, knowing things he had to drag out of her.

"What, Mona?"

"The intolerance," she replied in her own time. "He wanted to be all white. You want to be all Indian. As if there's no in between."

Hank's "wanna be" crack echoed in Joe's ears. "I am Ottawa," he said.

"You're both worlds. I told you that before when you asked my advice. You're denying yourself, Joe. Don't do it."

This time every word pierced its target. He wanted wisdom? It was hitting him full force. Susannah was part of him, the part he'd been trying to live down—just as surely as his father had denied his Ottawa blood. Susannah was a part he needed to be whole.

But other questions lingered. "What if she decides to leave somewhere down the line, after we have a child?"

Mona's hands didn't pause. Having gone through it herself, he sensed she'd braced herself for this one. "You do what you have to." She put her basket down and studied him. "I'm no fortune-teller, Joe. You do what's best for both of you. That's all you can ever do. Now make me some coffee. I'm tired of arguing common sense."

Twelve

Outside the tribal council meeting room, Susannah gathered her papers. It was a simple outline. It could be presented in fifteen minutes. If she didn't fall apart. Which she was about to.

She smoothed her linen skirt. Why had she worn linen on the hottest day of the year? The council met in a room that wasn't air-conditioned. By six o'clock it would be airless and humid, and she'd be a mass of wrinkles just sitting there waiting to be called on.

And watching Joe Bond from the front row.

Solution? Don't sit down and don't go in. Not yet.

They'd sent her a copy of the agenda. She was on later. She could stay in the hallway until after the first break.

She paced, took a drink from the fountain, nervously played with some hairpins, and ducked into the ladies' room to check out how the braid was holding up. She said hello to two women from the casino and wondered why they gave her such stiff smiles. Is this what Joe had been putting up with the last three weeks? Would they both be better off if she simply gave up?

Maybe. But she was going to give it one more try. Whether they were lovers or friends, they were going to be living in the same area. They needed to talk.

One look in the mirror, and she groaned. "Oh, Lord. No wonder they looked at you funny." Her face was puffy from the humidity. The light tan she'd managed at the beginning of the summer had faded to nothing but a pasty background for her freckles. She looked sticky. She felt worse.

She wanted this agony over with. If she couldn't convince Joe she meant to stay, she'd drop it. There was plenty of other work for her. She was busy making contracts, going after new accounts. But the bay wasn't so big, nor the marina so crowded, that she could fail to notice Joe's boat every day. Settling things with Joe would be decidedly easier than avoiding him. It would certainly take less energy.

"Sometimes life ain't easy, s—sugar." She paused and looked at her red-rimmed eyes. She'd almost said *squandeh*.

On the other hand, asking to make a presentation to the council was no guarantee she'd see Joe either. When she'd called William Missaukee, she knew there was every chance Joe would be out on his boat.

No such luck. *The Sporting Chance* was docked as she drove by the marina. He was there. This was her last chance to make any kind of impression. In the mirror, the nerve-racked woman with loose tendrils of red hair popping out of her French braid didn't inspire much confidence.

Despairing of fixing anything now, Susannah

stepped into the hallway. She closed her eyes and took three deep breaths.

"We're ready for you, Miss Moran."

She didn't even jump. That had to be a good sign. She was ready, she was in charge, she was in love. Now all she had to do was convince Joe that she had every intention of staying. She picked up her briefcase and went in.

A few council members looked up. Joe didn't.

William Missaukee read the information from the agenda. "For the record, we've been joined by Susannah Moran of the firm of Whitman, Jablonski, and Parritt. Whenever you'd like to begin, Miss Moran."

"Thank you." She had to take a sip of water first. It was tepid. Her hand shook, her heart pounded, and her face felt clammy. Her slip was sticking to the backs of her legs.

"I asked to be included today—"

Joe glanced up. Her voice caught.

"I asked to be included today—" It broke. "Excuse me." She took another drink of water. She would have taken another deep breath, but the thick, heavy air wasn't cooperating. Joe was looking at her openly now. She couldn't break down.

"As you may know, Whitman, Jablonski, and Parritt have opened an office on M-twenty-two, south of the reservation and just north of Sutton's Bay."

See, Joe? You expected me to run. I'm not going. I'm setting up a business.

"I've been appointed head of the new branch. I'd like to take this opportunity to assure you our work with the Grand Traverse Band of Ottawa and Chippewa Indians will continue uninterrupted. We believe a local office will allow better access to the services we can supply, for a deeper and more beneficial long-term relationship."

Long-term relationship. Like marriage, Joe. Like children.

Maybe she'd been too obvious with that last part. Joe returned her gaze for a long moment. His eyes were so blue. She couldn't have forgotten that in three weeks. Clear and unwavering, they shocked her with their intimacy.

And why shouldn't they? He'd seen everything there was to see of Susannah Moran. Except her stubborn streak. She took another sip of water and squared her shoulders.

"The main reason I asked to address tonight's council meeting was to present to you the outline of the Gerald R. Whitman Scholarship Program. This is open to high school students wishing to go on to college to major in accounting or business-related fields. We've opened it to any member of the community under the age of eighteen, to help defray college expenses."

I can help make things better here too, Joe.

"How the young man or woman is chosen would be up to the council. The copies you have show a number of methods that have been used in the past, from essay writing to speech contests to a simple recommendation from the council."

But I can offer only so much. The next move is up to you.

"If you have any questions, I'll be happy to answer them now." And happy to sit down. Her heart was hammering. The tepid water tasted of minerals, the glass of soapsuds. A standing fan moved little more than the plastic streamers tied to it. If they didn't get some air in there, she'd faint.

"Thank you, Miss Moran. We'll look it over and discuss it further at the next meeting."

That was it? Susannah was prepared to answer questions now. She rose, her legs and every other part of her shaking. At least her voice was under control. "Uh, thank you, Mr. Missaukee. I'd like to thank the council for this opportunity and for their time."

She found her briefcase somehow. It banged against the back of her chair in her rush to leave, popping open and spilling papers everywhere. "Excuse me." She crouched to scoop them back in.

No one helped. Everyone seemed to be waiting for someone else to jump in. He didn't.

"Sorry," she said. All right, it was humiliating. But she would not burst into tears. Not until she got to the car. Briefcase clamped under her arm, she blindly made her way down the aisle.

Joe stared at the paperwork in front of him. She looked awful. Pale. Her voice shook. She drank water as if they were surrounded by a desert instead of the Great Lakes. She looked gray and nauseated.

She looked like she had a prize case of morning sickness.

William was discussing possible topics for the essay contest. "Excuse me," Joe said.

He ran down the aisle after Susannah.

No one seemed surprised.

He frantically searched the parking lot. Her car was there. She wasn't. That's when he caught sight of her slipping into the woods at the back of the lot. He would walk, not run, after her. A dozen thoughts clawed at him. What if she were carrying his baby? What if she'd wanted to stay all along, and he'd chased her away? What if he'd made his own nightmare come true?

"Susannah!"

It was like stalking a deer, a sprite, a ghost. The neutral linen faded in and out of the trees, heavy and dark with summer growth.

"Susannah!"

Mona had been right about his being of both worlds. He had to learn to live with both. With Susannah he'd felt settled. And unsettled. And crazy with want and longing and loneliness. Now he felt scared.

He thought he'd needed time.

He needed a good swift kick in the pants.

Something moved in the trees. They were almost at the top of the hill, the one where they'd kissed so long ago.

"Susannah."

She turned. Her eyes were puffy, her face tear-stained. "Sorry. I don't enjoy making a fool of myself in public."

"Or over me?"

She bit her lip, clutching the damn briefcase to her chest as if it were a shield. He was always too blunt, too honest. She'd been trying to pretend she was upset over some spilled papers. She wiped the tears away, not caring about smeared makeup. "What are you looking at?"

"I have to know."

"What?" she replied bleakly, ready to tell him for the hundredth time that she loved him, that she would stay, if only he'd ask.

"Are you pregnant?" he demanded instead.

It took a moment for the question to sink in. Sailboats glided over the water below. Spinnakers filled their bellies with wind. Oh, how she'd love to be pregnant! With his child. But he seemed more angry than pleased, and besides, it wasn't true.

He gripped her arms. "Tell me."

"Joe," she said, swallowing tears, composing what little there was left to compose, "we've always been very careful. You don't have to worry about that now."

"There was one time, in the water."

She remembered. It was all so painfully clear. She'd spent weeks going over every moment. She shook her head. "I'm not."

"But you could be."

"But I'm not! It's been over three weeks, Joe. I know."

She gave up and sat down. She didn't care about the sandy ground, or the linen suit, or even whether he believed her. She pulled her knees up to her chest and looked out at the water. "Is that all you wanted to know? Whether there were any loose ends to tie up? Don't worry, you're a free man."

Hardly free, Joe knew—not of his past, nor of her. He could do nothing about the past. If he was lucky, it might not be too late for them. He sat down opposite her and studied her profile, his back against a tree.

"What would you do if you were?" he asked quietly, snapping a twig between his fingers. He tossed it aside and waited for her answer.

"I'd have it."

"Would you tell me?"

"Of course. It'd be yours. You'd have a right to know."

"And to keep it?"

"I don't know how we'd work that out." He was talking about custody, not marriage. "I live only down the road."

"You could move away."

"And maybe I could jump off this cliff and fly.

Who's to say, all right?" She was suddenly fed up. "You're always so quick to see the negative. Do you really have such a harsh opinion of me?"

All those words his father drummed into his head echoed in his mind and retreated like thunder. "Not you, *ninimoshe*, me. My father taught me to be white, my mother to be Ottawa. I've never tried being both. Ironic when you think about it, since that's what I am."

She watched the light dappling his dark skin, his blue eyes like patches of sky. "Do you want to be both?"

"I'm learning. It isn't easy. I'm afraid the past will repeat itself, that I'll make the mistakes my father did."

"You don't have to."

"No. I can see that now." In her eyes.

He reached for her and they stood, his arms slipping naturally around her waist. Her arms were around his neck before she could stop them. They belonged there.

He handed her a handkerchief.

"You could at least ask me," she sniffed.

"Why are you crying?"

"Not that." She swiped at his knit shirt with the handkerchief, then blew her nose. "But I want you to ask me when my nose isn't swollen and my eyes aren't bloodshot. I want to look beautiful."

"You always do."

"Thanks, but that's not what I want to hear."

He grinned at her pout and put a finger to her lips. "Shh, *ninimoshe*." He had to stop her now, before she did all the asking. The woman was entirely too generous and open-hearted, too willing to try. "Don't you want me to tell you how sexy you are? Isn't that the way marriage stays fresh?"

"I wouldn't know. I haven't heard a lot about

marriages succeeding lately." She pushed herself out of his arms. Standing before him, she straightened her shoulders and cleared her throat. That didn't prevent her eyes from tearing up no matter how furiously she blinked. "I love you, Joe. I want you to know that before you say another word. And I intend to stay no matter what. I want a home, a real one, even if I have to make it myself."

He nodded his head slowly. Then he took her hand between his as if he intended to put a ring on it right there. His eyes twinkled. "If you want to build a home yourself, I've seen some good log designs." He lifted her hand to his lips and nibbled her knuckles.

"I wasn't talking construction techniques!"

His rumbling chuckle agreed. A weight was lifting from her shoulders. The horizon was becoming clear. But Susannah had to have it spelled out.

"I mean a home the two of us make, no matter what our differences. I can't be what I'm not. I can't be Ottawa."

"You can take my breath away, *squandeh*. Don't change that." His hand was in her hair. Her heart was in her throat. "My life is here," he said, "and so is my wife."

She ran a finger down the open collar of his shirt. "*Our* life, *ninimoshe*. And don't you forget it." A quick tug on his collar, and his mouth came down to hers.

The kiss was tender, full of remembrance. Apologies were given, accepted, and passed over. Sparks were struck. Everything they'd missed, everything they had yet to look forward to, was there.

"Mmmm." Susannah could barely breathe. In fact, his arms were so tight around her, she'd forgotten when she'd last drawn air. Reaching her arms behind her to loosen his grip at her back, she pressed her breasts against him.

"Does that hurt?" he asked.

"You're stronger than you know."

"I'm learning."

"Strong can also mean controlling your temper. I've never told you how much I admired your standing up to Keith without bopping him one."

"Jealousy may not be a pretty emotion, but I never want to hear his name again. Okay?"

The sparkle in her eyes said she wasn't taking him nearly seriously enough. Pursing her lips and turning an imaginary key was no way to promise eternal silence.

"He has nothing to do with operations out in the boondocks," she replied. "I think one visit was enough."

"Good. I was ready to tie an anchor to his ankle and drop him off Deepwater Point."

Susannah smiled impishly. "Mmm wimps mr reeled."

"What?"

"My lips are sealed."

"Super Glue would do better."

"Ha! You think I'm going to stop giving you a hard time just because we're married?"

"Might be wise."

"You have a wife who stands her ground. Aren't you lucky?"

"So I've noticed."

She had one hand saucily cocked on her hip, the other was spearheaded by a red fingernail at point-blank range just above his heart. Susannah wistfully realized the question of "will you marry me" had been answered without ever being asked. She also realized she could live with that.

Joe had another question. "Will all our children have their mother's fiery temper?"

"They might have her hair," she responded carefully, watching his reaction.

"And their father's blue eyes."

They laughed at the irony. Smile met smile, better because it was shared.

Susannah made a show of leaning back to appraise Joe's features. "If I had a daughter with your cheekbones, I'd be a truly happy woman. What a knockout. You'll be chasing the boys away."

"I have a harpoon somewhere. What about a son with your freckles?"

"What about ten, each a different combination?"

"Mongrels," he muttered, the teasing back in his eyes.

She scowled and poked him in the ribs. "They'll be pieces of you and me."

"That's one way to look at it."

"That's the truth, Mr. Bond." She tugged at the back of his head and brought his mouth down to hers.

"Is this your way of telling me I'm thinking too much?" Joe asked after catching his breath.

"Mmm-hmmm."

"Maybe we should get started and see what we get."

"Unh-unh. I have an office to get off the ground. And a condo to furnish. For two. And clothes to buy."

"I've rarely seen you in the same thing twice."

"I was thinking of nightwear." She wrapped a finger around a buttonhole at the base of his neck. "I can't start married life sleeping in oversize T-shirts."

"Is that what you wear? I've never noticed."

"I've never worn them around you."

He swallowed, his Adam's apple bobbing against her fingertip as it further investigated the V of his shirt.

"Around you, I've worn very little at all."

"Let's keep it that way." He tugged her off the path and into a flourishing fence of lilac bushes, claiming her mouth as if they had no time to lose.

Susannah's sigh was long and delicious. His mouth was the most delectable meal she'd ever tasted. "Joseph Louis Bond," she murmured hazily.

"How'd you find all that out?"

"Loan records from the economic development files."

"Accountants are snoops."

"I won't deny it. Where are we going?"

"To the top of the hill." His voice was muffled, his mouth occupied with that pale strip of skin behind her ear. Why did she hide it behind all that hair when it had to be the sexiest part on her body? But that wasn't counting her lips, her breasts, that freckle behind her knee that made her wild every time he kissed it.

He had to get his thoughts off her body long enough to formulate a coherent sentence. When he saw the humor and love in her eyes, and thought how close he'd come to driving her out of his life, it was even harder. "We're going up there, where I kissed you the first time. But this time it'll be a little more private."

"Ahh."

"I'm going to propose there."

"Oh."

"Since we've already decided where we'll live and how many children we're going to have, I thought I'd better get the marriage part nailed down."

"Very sensible." Unlike the way she was feeling as he peered into her eyes.

"When we get there," he said, his voice suddenly hoarse, "I'm going to make love to you."

She glanced up. Her heart was fluttering and her legs felt too weak to support her much longer. "It's a very tall hill."

"I like the view." He liked the way her nipples tightened under her blouse and her skin flushed. He took her face in his hands. "Susannah."

"Yes, my love." Her eyes were alight with happiness.

"You will marry me," he said sternly. It was the only way to get around the tightness in his throat.

"I will."

"And you'll never leave."

Although her face was trapped between his hands, she shook her head forcefully.

"You won't take the children."

"All ten of them? They'd never fit in the Porsche." He scowled.

"Just kidding. I'll only take them to visit their grandparents. And on a couple of trips to Chicago." She quickly countered his frown.

"For sight-seeing and skyscrapers. Besides, no childhood would be complete without a visit to Marshall Field. This will be their home, Joe. And mine."

"Will it?"

"Between the sage advice of their father on the council and the economic brilliance of their mother, they'll have a home they can be very proud of. I already am." She kissed him softly but thoroughly. "Better build us a big house."

"I plan to. With a master bedroom looking out on the bay."

Susannah watched the water glittering below. Just like on their first visit there, Joe knew he'd rather look at her, sparkling, laughing, giving his life meaning, looking up into his eyes.

She ran a hand down his chest. It made her voice breathless, her heart race. But it was nothing like the sensations he caused in her, unbuttoning her blouse one button at a time. He drew it back over her shoulders. "A kiss shouldn't end at the neck."

"No?"

Her hands were wrapped in his black hair, his head dipping lower, trailing kisses, tugging at one breast then the other until they were both on their knees, the sandy ground shifting, accommodating.

"How many children did we agree on?" Susannah asked.

"Ten."

"Maybe we *should* get started."

"*Ninimoshe*, we already have."

Epilogue

The music of the powwow thrummed up through the soles of Susannah's feet. She wiggled her toes in her moccasins. Although they didn't match the maternity jumper, they were the best thing she'd found for swollen feet.

"How's it going, Mona?"

"Going good," her mother-in-law replied. "Be happy when it's over, and I can go back to working instead of selling. I'm no salesman."

Susannah laughed doubtfully. "The first time I met you I walked away with seven baskets."

"You still have them?"

"You know we do."

"Then talk to this lady here. Tell her what good work I do."

"You need no help from me," Susannah replied, laughing as she waved good-bye.

She placed a hand on her swollen belly and sighed. Her back ached. It was going to be a hot afternoon, but the powwow was a great success.

There were more than a dozen craft displays. Tribes from all over the state were participating.

The dancing never stopped. She was surrounded by murmurings in languages she caught only in bits and pieces. But she could honestly say she'd never felt more completely at home. This was her community, where she belonged.

"How's my beautiful wife?"

"Just about to find a chair." She took Joe's arm, and they moved toward the ring of chairs outlining the central area.

"Tired?" he asked.

"How did you guess?"

He steered her to a seat. "William wants me over at the development booth. I told him I had a higher priority."

"Bet I know who she is," Susannah teased.

People filled the center of the meeting ground. Music began, as rhythmic and eternal as the singing that accompanied it. Moccasined feet made a shuffling sound on the grass, like deer rustling through trees. Beads sewn decoratively onto leather clicked and swayed, adding their own percussion.

Women's voices took up the chant. They formed a circle within the circle, then two rows. The girls came in, their voices reedy and high.

"Here she comes," Joe said, his mouth taut with expectation.

"My rival," Susannah replied, taking his hand.

A dark-haired little girl came to the front of the line. Her voice was like a piping bird in the forest, her skin like polished cherry wood. A black braid fell down her back, entwined with feathers. Big brown eyes glanced at the audience. Eyes like her mother's.

"She's beautiful, Red."

"Striking."

The little girl added a step, then looked to see if anyone caught it.

"And a shameless flirt," Susannah added, hiding a smile.

"Wonder where she gets that?" Joe laughed. But his earthy, teasing look that should have made her smile made Susannah's heart thrum instead.

He put his hand on her belly and hers closed over it. "Boy or girl?" he asked gruffly.

"Wait and see."

His piercing look put fire in her veins, joining with the building music, like the primitive rhythm that had carried them away the night Lucy had been conceived. A flush rose to her cheeks. It had been five years, and she still desired him more than ever.

He squeezed her hand, reading her thoughts. "I love you," he said in Ottawa.

That phrase she knew by heart. She'd heard it every day and each night of those five years. She knew it as surely as she knew Lucy's Indian name, the one Joe picked. The Flame That Never Dies.

THE EDITOR'S CORNER

Those sultry June breezes will soon start to whisper through the trees, bringing with them the wonderful scents of summer. Imagine the unmistakable aroma of fresh-cut grass and the feeling of walking barefoot across a lush green lawn. Then look on your bookstore shelves for our striking jade-green LOVESWEPTs! The beautiful covers next month will put you right in the mood to welcome the summer season—and our authors will put you in the mood for romance.

Peggy Webb weaves her sensual magic once more in **UNTIL MORNING COMES**, LOVESWEPT #402. In this emotional story, Peggy captures the stark beauty of the Arizona desert and the fragile beauty of the love two very different people find together. In San Francisco he's known as Dr. Colter Gray, but in the land of his Apache ancestors, he's Gray Wolf. Reconciling the two aspects of his identity becomes a torment to Colter, but when he meets Jo Beth McGill, his life heads in a new direction. Jo Beth has brought her elderly parents along on her assignment to photograph the desert cacti. Concerned about her father's increasing senility, Jo Beth has vowed never to abandon her parents to the perils of old age. But when she meets Colter, she worries that she'll have to choose between them. When Colter appears on his stallion in the moonlight, ready to woo her with ancient Apache love rituals, Jo Beth trembles with excitement and gives herself up to the mysterious man in whose arms she finds her own security. This tender story deals with love on many levels and will leave you with a warm feeling in your heart.

In LOVESWEPT #403 by Linda Cajio, all it takes is **JUST ONE LOOK** for Remy St. Jacques to fall for the beguiling seductress Susan Kitteridge. Ordered to shadow the woman he believes to be a traitor, Remy comes to realize the lady who drives him to sweet obsession could not be what she seemed. Afraid of exposing those she loves to danger, Susan is caught up in the life of lies she'd live for so long. But she yearns to confess all to Remy the moment the bayou outlaw captures her lips with his. In her smooth, sophisticated style, Linda creates a winning love story you won't be able to put down. As an added treat, Linda brings back the lovable character of Lettice as her third and last granddaughter finds true happiness and love. Hint! Hint! This won't be the last you'll hear of Lettice, though. Stay tuned!

(continued)

With her debut book, **PERFECT MORNING**, published in April 1989, Marcia Evanick made quite a splash in the romance world. Next month Marcia returns to the LOVESWEPT lineup with **INDESCRIBABLY DELICIOUS**, LOVESWEPT #404. Marcia has a unique talent for blending the sensuality of a love story with the humorous trials and tribulations of single parenthood. When Dillon McKenzie follows a tantalizing scent to his neighbor's kitchen, he finds delicious temptation living next door! Elizabeth Lancaster is delighted that Dillon and his two sons have moved in; now her boy Aaron will have playmates. What she doesn't count on is becoming Dillon's playmate! He brings out all her hidden desires and makes her see there's so much more to life than just her son and the business she's built creating scrumptious cakes and candies. You'll be enthralled by these two genuine characters who must find a way to join their families as well as their dreams.

As promised, Tami Hoag returns with her second pot of pure gold in *The Rainbow Chasers* series, **KEEPING COMPANY**, LOVESWEPT #405. Alaina Montgomery just knew something would go wrong on her way to her friend Jayne's costume party dressed as a sexy comic-book princess. When her car konks out on a deserted stretch of road, she's more embarrassed by her costume than frightened of danger—until Dylan Harrison stops to help her. At first she believes he's an escaped lunatic, then he captivates her with his charm and incredible sex appeal—and Alaina actually learns to like him—even after he gets them arrested. A cool-headed realist, Alaina is unaccustomed to Dylan's care-free attitude toward life. So she surprises even herself when she accepts his silly proposal to "keep company" to curtail their matchmaking friends from interfering in their lives. Even more surprising is the way Dylan makes her feel, as if her mouth were made for long, slow kisses. Tami's flare for humor shines in this story of a reckless dreamer who teaches a lady lawyer to believe in magic.

In Judy Gill's **DESPERADO**, LOVESWEPT #406, hero Bruce Hagendorn carries the well-earned nickname of Stud. But there's much more to the former hockey star than his name implies—and he intends to convince his lovely neighbor, Mary Delaney, of that fact. After Mary saves him from a severe allergy attack that she had unintentionally caused, Bruce vows to coax his personal Florence Nightingale out to play. An intensely driven woman, Mary has set certain goals

(continued)

for herself that she's focused all her attention on attaining—doing so allows her to shut out the hurts from her past. But Bruce/Stud won't take no for an answer, and Mary finds herself caught under the spell of the most virile man she's ever met. She can't help wishing, though, that he'd tell her where he goes at night, what kind of business it is that he's so dedicated to. But Bruce knows once he tells Mary, he could lose her forever. This powerful story is sure to have an impact on the lives of many readers, as Judy deals with the ecstasy and the heartache true love can bring.

We're delighted as always to bring you another memorable romance from one of the ladies who's helped make LOVESWEPT so successful. Fayrene Preston's *SwanSea Place:* **DECEIT,** LOVESWEPT #407, is the *pièce de résistance* to a fabulous month of romantic reading awaiting you. Once again Fayrene transports you to Maine and the great estate of SwanSea Place, where Richard Zagen has come in search of Liana Marchall, the only woman he's ever loved. Richard has been haunted, tormented by memories of the legendary model he knows better as the heartless siren who'd left him to build her career in the arms of another. Liana knows only too well the desperate desire Richard is capable of making her feel. She's run once from the man who could give her astonishing pleasure and inflict shattering pain, but time has only deepened her hunger for him. Fayrene's characters create more elemental force than the waves crashing against the rocky coast. Let them sweep you up in their inferno of passion!

As always we invite you to write to us with your thoughts and comments. We hope your summer is off to a fabulous start! Sincerely,

Susann Brailey

Susann Brailey
Editor
LOVESWEPT
Bantam Books
666 Fifth Avenue
New York, NY 10103

FAN OF THE MONTH

Ricki L. Ebbs

I guess I started reading the LOVESWEPT series as soon as it hit the market. I had been looking for a different kind of romance novel, one that had humor, adventure, a little danger, some offbeat characters, and, of course, true love and a happy ending. When I read my first LOVESWEPT, I stopped looking.

Fayrene Preston, Kay Hooper, Iris Johansen, Joan Elliott Pickart, Sandra Brown, and Deborah Smith are some of my favorite authors. I love Kay Hooper's wonderful sense of humor. For pure sensuality, Sandra Brown's books are unsurpassed. Though their writing styles are different, Iris Johansen, Joan Elliott Pickart, and Fayrene Preston write humorous, touching, and wonderfully sentimental stories. Deborah Smith's books have a unique blend of adventure and romance, and she keeps bringing back those characters I always wonder about at the end of the story. (I'm nosy about my friends' lives too.)

I'm single, with a terrific but demanding job as an administrative assistant. When I get the chance, I always pick up a mystery or romance novel. I have taken some kidding from my family and friends for my favorite reading. My brother says I should have been Sherlock Holmes or Scarlett O'Hara. I don't care what they say. I may be one of the last romantics, but I think the world looks a little better with a slightly romantic tint, and LOVESWEPTs certainly help to keep it rosy.

60 Minutes to a Better, More Beautiful You!

Now it's easier than ever to awaken your sensuality, stay slim forever—even make yourself irresistible. With Bantam's bestselling subliminal audio tapes, you're only 60 minutes away from a better, more beautiful you!

THE DELANEY DYNASTY

THE SHAMROCK TRINITY

☐   21975   RAFE, THE MAVERICK
     by Kay Hooper $2.95

☐   21976   YORK, THE RENEGADE
     by Iris Johansen $2.95

☐   21977   BURKE, THE KINGPIN
     by Fayrene Preston $2.95

THE DELANEYS OF KILLAROO

☐   21872   ADELAIDE, THE ENCHANTRESS
     by Kay Hooper $2.75

☐   21873   MATILDA, THE ADVENTURESS
     by Iris Johansen $2.75

☐   21874   SYDNEY, THE TEMPTRESS
     by Fayrene Preston $2.75

THE DELANEYS: *The Untamed Years*

☐   21899   GOLDEN FLAMES *by Kay Hooper* $3.50

☐   21898   WILD SILVER *by Iris Johansen* $3.50

☐   21897   COPPER FIRE *by Fayrene Preston* $3.50

THE DELANEYS II

☐   21978   SATIN ICE *by Iris Johansen* $3.50

☐   21979   SILKEN THUNDER *by Fayrene Preston* $3.50

☐   21980   VELVET LIGHTNING *by Kay Hooper* $3.50